I0445703

A DECEMBER WISH

TRACY BROEMMER

A December Wish

by

Tracy Broemmer

Contemporary Romance

Published by Tracy Broemmer

Edited by Lexie Broemmer

Cover by No Sweat Graphics & Formatting

All Rights Reserved

Copyright © 2023

ISBN#: 978-1-951637-77-4

Names, characters, and incidents depicted in this book are products of the author's imagination or are used fictitiously. Any resemblance to actual events, or person, living or dead, is coincidental and not the intent of the author.

No part of this book may be reproduced or transmitted in any form or by any means without permission in writing from the author.

For the people who make the holidays magical

~for me, it was my mom

CHAPTER ONE

THE SNOW STARTED IN EARNEST WHEN HE EXITED FROM I-35N TO US-36 around Colfax Township in Missouri—roughly an hour after Drake Palmer left Overland Park to head for Champaign. He wasn't one to worry about driving in snow which was why he had ignored the dire winter weather advisory. Now here he was two or three hours in, smack in the middle of coming and going, surrounded by cars—even some that he would have assumed were all-wheel drive, if not four-wheel drive—off the road. A few of them had completely jumped the median and were turned around on the wrong side of the highway.

Drake eyed one such economy-sized car as traffic on his side of the highway crept along at a turtle's speed. Enough snow had fallen on said car that he couldn't make out much about it, other than that it was red. What he could deduce from seeing so many cars off the road and the rate at which he now drove was that this particular area had already had some ice before the deluge of snow had started.

He tried to read the highway signs, but it was hard to see with the ice and snow glaze covering them. If he had read the last one correctly, he was near Monroe City, Missouri. Probably, he should be sensible and pull off when he came to that exit. But he wouldn't. His meeting in Champaign might end up delayed if that part of Illinois was getting hit like Missouri was, but he still just wanted to get there. As long as he played it safe, he should be okay.

"Hey, Siri," he said as he turned the Christmas music playing in his car down a bit.

"Uh-huh." Siri's smooth female voice said as the colorful prompt lit up on his phone screen.

"How far is Monroe City from Hannibal, Missouri?"

It wasn't as if he hadn't driven this road a million times, as if he couldn't drive it in his sleep. But he was getting tired, the blowing snow was creating blizzard-like conditions, and he might need to plan ahead. Maybe he wasn't going to make it all the way to Champaign, Illinois, but if he was careful, he might be able to make it just over the state line. Which he knew was somewhere in the middle of the river on the other side of Hannibal.

"Hannibal, Missouri is about twenty-two miles from Monroe City, Missouri, by car."

Drake eyed the road in front of him again. He could make it another twenty-two miles. He would just have to be vigilant. To that end, he kept the music turned down so low he could barely hear it. His phone buzzed a couple of times with texts, but he didn't bother with looking at them.

The drive wasn't particularly exciting on a good day. Creeping along so slowly, so cautiously, only made it that much more boring. Finally, though, Drake reached Hannibal. Thankfully, the main road through the town was somewhat clear. Slow and steady, he steered his SUV along US-36. Traffic was a bit lighter in town, which surprised him. Seemed like the Wednesday before Christmas traffic would be crazier in town with people shopping for gifts and groceries, especially with the snowstorm. He would have thought holiday travel would have started closer to the weekend.

Drake wouldn't admit it to his brothers or buddies, but he held his breath as he inched over the bridge across the Mississippi. If he was going to wreck in the storm, he would prefer to do that on land and not over the river. His headlights lit a swath of snow-covered trees as he drove off the bridge onto solid ground in Illinois. It was pretty; his mom would love to see the trees, the freshly fallen snow on the fields.

Except if she knew he was driving in the storm, she would threaten him within an inch of his life. No matter that he was a thirty-three-year-old man. As the mother of three boys, Vicky Palmer had well-used and very efficient mom voice. She would let him have it.

So he wouldn't tell her. He would get to Champaign, attend his meeting, and head back home. His family would be none the wiser.

Drake groaned a bit when he felt his front tires slide a bit.

"Not now," he mumbled. He was less than thirty minutes from Quincy, Illinois. If he could get to Quincy safely, he would stop there for the night. He glanced at the clock on his dash. Seven-thirty. *Perfect.* He would arrive in Quincy late enough that he shouldn't have to wait to get a table or a seat at a bar for a quick dinner and then he would get a hotel.

His mom would be proud of him once he was back home. Sure, she'd give him hell for crossing the bridge in blizzard conditions, but she would be happy he had stopped in Quincy.

The car slid a bit again. Drake gripped the steering wheel hard, but suddenly, he was spinning. Thoughts of all the cars off the road he had seen on the trek from Monroe City to Hannibal, he tapped the brakes and held his breath.

Raised Catholic, he wasn't one to think much about God or heaven or death, even. But as his SUV spun out of control and he flew off the highway, the SUV turning on its side, he wondered about all three.

The sound of screeching metal pierced the quiet interior of the vehicle. Drake was belted in, so even though he was jerked around a bit, and he bumped his head hard enough to see stars for a second, he thought he was okay. He held tight to the steering wheel as the SUV skidded deep into the drop-off past the shoulder. At least he hadn't gone into the oncoming lane of traffic.

Finally, the awful screeching stopped. The SVU had stopped. Drake sat for a moment, blinking at the sideways snow-covered trees in front of him. The seatbelt held him in, but his whole body pressed heavily to the right side. If he unbuckled now, he was going to crash into the passenger seat.

He had to, though, didn't he? To take stock. See if he was hurt more seriously than he'd first thought. To see how bad the vehicle was.

Right, Drake. Because what? You're going to flip it back over and drive it on into Quincy?

"Let me just summon some superhero strength," he mumbled. The thought was so ridiculous, he laughed out loud. Oddly enough his phone was still in the holder on the vent by the steering wheel. Drake tapped his fingers on the seatbelt, considering what to do first. Call for help or unfasten the belt.

He grabbed the phone and tapped the screen. He would call for help.

Except he was in that spot here with no cell coverage. He had driven through this area often on business. How many calls had dropped on this stretch of road?

With a frustrated sigh, Drake put the phone down in the cup holder and then cursed when it rattled around and fell to the floor on the passenger side. Bracing himself, he pushed the release on his seatbelt. His body slumped toward the passenger seat, but he caught himself.

Now what?

He would have to get familiar with those prayers he had learned as a boy. And pray that someone came along and offered to help.

CHAPTER TWO

Kynlee Austin gritted her teeth as Mariah Carey's voice surrounded her in the small grocery store. She'd heard the song four times already this morning, and frankly, right now, all she wanted for Christmas was to never hear it again. Even worse? Seemed like everyone she saw here in Berry's was singing along.

Casualty of where she lived, she supposed. Although, how in the world there was a small town in midwestern Illinois named Reindeer Meadow, she had no idea. Oh, Kynlee was well aware of the history, the lore, but it made no sense to her. She liked the Fayrweather family well enough, and she assumed Elmer and Lydia Fayrweather—the family said to have settled here and started the tree farm, the *magic*— were as nice as Harold and Edna Fayrweather, the fifth generation to run the farm.

Illinois was teeming with deer, but not *reindeer*. So, the fact that Elmer and Lydia plucked the name *Reindeer Meadow* out of thin air when they settled the small town made no sense to Kynlee. And because everyone who lived here loved

Christmas and tended to be festive all year long, it irritated her, too.

Don't even get her started on that old tale of magic at the Fayrweather Tree Farm.

"Hey, Kynlee."

She nodded at the woman who slipped past her to get to the dairy cooler. Reindeer Meadow boasted a population of three thousand, but the number fluctuated. Joe Donahue passed away last April, but then Eric and Deanna Hooper had triplets in June. Didn't matter, though. Everyone tended to know everyone here, at least by sight or name. For the most part, most people knew everyone else's business, too.

Kynlee set her box of donuts and the jug of milk on the conveyor belt at the checkout as the song changed to something less irritating than Mariah Carey's exceptionally popular "All I Want for Christmas Is You." But John Denver singing "The Christmas Song" was still a Christmas song. Kynlee offered Joanie Kassens a smile and did her best to still the tension digging into her neck and shoulders, like animal claws clenching pretty.

"Few more days," Joanie told her as she handed over a twenty to pay for her stuff.

Joanie, like everyone else in Reindeer Meadow, was aware that Kynlee wasn't a fan of Christmas.

"Yep." Kynlee nodded. "Gettin' there."

"How's your mom and dad doing?" Joanie counted back her change.

"Good." Like everyone else in town, her parents, her sister, and her brother-in-law, all loved the holiday season. Despite that, she was close to all of them. Her smile was genuine now; her parents owned a landscaping business in town. They were well-loved by everyone. Her sister Holly was a second-grade teacher at Immaculate Conception school—also well-loved by everyone.

Kynlee didn't often consider how the people in Reindeer Meadow viewed her. She was relatively polite, courteous. Hardworking. Generous.

But she had heard the bah-humbugs muttered behind her back a time or two.

"Tell them hello for me."

"Will do." She picked up the box of donuts and jug of milk to head out the door, slowing her steps when the automatic doors swished open. Calvin Grady stomped his feet on the mat as he entered the store. The old man's cheeks and nose were rosy red. Maybe like Santa Claus, Kynlee thought, if there was such a person.

"Hey, Calvin!" Joanie called to him. The old man turned his attention their way. He waved and offered Kynlee a smile. "What's going on today?"

"Got a live one," he answered, his voice charged and happy. Kynlee thought again of all the silly Christmas movies about Santa Claus and gave herself a mental shake.

"Yeah?" Joanie leaned her back on her cash register and folded her arms over her chest. "What's up?"

"Found an SUV off the road around eight last night." Calvin shook his head. "Darn kids, always in such a hurry."

"They okay?" Joanie asked what Kynlee was thinking.

Calvin shrugged, but he nodded. "Banged up a bit. I found him when I was out plowing the roads. Good thing, too. No cell service out there."

"Where was he headed?"

"Says he was coming from Overland Park," Calvin told Kynlee. "On the way to Champaign."

"He crossed the bridge in a blizzard?" She snorted. There was a word for someone like that. Idiot came to mind.

"Well, thankfully, he got over the bridge okay," Calvin answered. "Gave him a lift. Left him at Cecil's. I imagine the guy's gonna need to see the doc today just to be sure he's okay."

"Yeah." Kynlee agreed. "Maybe he should have a scan to see if he has a brain."

Joanie and Calvin both chuckled at Kynlee's acerbic comment.

"See ya later." She included them both in a wave and headed back outside. Too late, she decided she should have zipped her Carhartt coat up again. The snow had eased somewhat, but the brutal wind could still slice right through a person. Huddling deep inside the coat, she tucked her chin and headed north up the block to the rec room. Reindeer Meadow wasn't big enough for a YMCA, and not everyone here could get to Hannibal or Quincy easily, even on a good day. So, when Reindeer Meadow Elementary was built a few years back—one big building to accommodate most of the kids in the area—and the older, smaller school buildings had closed, the community had voted to keep one open as a community recreation center.

Tax money Kynlee didn't mind paying. Kids needed a safe space to hang out, to have fun, the exercise, dance, do homework—whatever the case may be.

"Excuse me." A tallish, solid-looking guy sidestepped her on the sidewalk. Kynlee noted his loafers and wool coat. And the small gash on his forehead. She glanced back at him as she walked. Might be good-looking, but if he was the idiot who had tried to make a six-hour drive during a blizzard, she would do well to keep walking.

At the rec center, with her hands full, she bumped the big, heavy door with her hip. The familiar groan greeted her as the door opened, followed quickly by the sounds of top forty music and girls giggling.

She loved top forty music about as much as Christmas music, but the giggles warmed her heart.

"Donuts anyone?" she called as she stepped inside the cavernous gymnasium.

"Kynlee!"

The squeal went up—seven voices combined to one very shrill, ear-piercing shriek. With a laugh, she put the box and the jug on the stage and pulled her black beanie off.

"Easy, girls," she cautioned them. "You guys could break glass with that shriek."

The girls surrounded her as she shrugged out of her coat and laid it and the beanie on the stage. Under the coat, she wore a black long-sleeved t-shirt and skinny jeans. Her sister had always been the girly one; Kynlee was a self-proclaimed tomboy. But she knew how to accessorize any outfit; today she wore a stack of bangle bracelets on her right arm and a chunky silver ring on her left hand.

Outdoorsy and athletic, Kynlee knew sometimes people made inaccurate assumptions about her. But she shrugged that off, along with the grinchette nickname she had earned before she made it out of grade school. Easy-going and adventurous, as long as those adventures were grounded in reality, she considered herself fun to hang out with.

"Dig in." She nodded at the donuts and stepped back when the girls—all smelling of fruity lotions and perfumes—rushed the stage.

CHAPTER THREE

Dr. Vanderburg patched up the gash on his forehead. Poked and prodded a few sore spots and decided Drake was going to live. The genteel older man offered him pain pills, but Drake opted for Tylenol. The doctor had offered him coffee, too, but the man had hinted that the coffee was better down the block at Frosty's.

Christmas-lover that he was, Drake decided if he was going to be stranded in a small town called Reindeer Meadow three days before Christmas, he was going to Frosty's for coffee. The walk from the small brick bungalow turned doctor's office to the café was brisk and chilly, but Drake didn't mind it. In fact, if he wasn't worried about his SUV, still on its side and covered in snow on the side of Highway Fifty-Seven for all he knew, he would enjoy the morning walk.

Frosty's turned out to be a small café decked out for the holidays as one would expect in this town. Drake approved; if he lived here, he would play up everything about the holidays and the name of the town, too. So far everyone he'd met here had been warm and friendly, a little bit like he was on the set of a Christmas movie.

When he tugged the door of the café open, he was immediately swallowed by heat and the smell of something baking. Not even aware that he was hungry, he laughed out loud when his stomach growled. A long slate grey counter lined the front of the place, ten stools—seven of which were taken—in front of the counter. A few two-top and four-top tables were scattered in the small open area, and there were a few cozy-looking chairs and loveseats gathered here and there for seating, too.

All those seats taken, Drake approached the counter, eyes on the chalkboard menu on the wall behind it. Perfectly printed letters formed words like sugar cookie, gingerbread men, coffee cake, and pecan pie. His stomach rumbled again as he unbuttoned his coat. The woman behind the counter greeted him with a smile, told him she would be right with him.

Drake looked around the place again and moved to the rack by the door to hang his coat before claiming a stool.

"I'm guessing you're not from around here." The woman tipped her head at him as she stood across the counter.

"Gee, how'd you guess?" he asked with a laugh. "Did the bandage on my head give it away?"

She laughed softly. "Yeah, but the coat..." She shrugged.

"What's wrong with my coat?" he yelped, sounding defensive.

"Nothing. We just don't see a lot of wool coats here. Mostly Carhartts and big parkas."

"Mmm." He nodded as he sat down. "Okay."

"I'm Liz," she announced and offered her hand. Drake shook it with a smile.

"Drake."

"What can I get you?"

Drake tipped his head back to study the board again. "Well, I need coffee. Dr. Vanderburg recommended your coffee over his."

"That's because Dottie makes it very weak," she whispered.

"Who's Dottie?"

"His receptionist. Who should have retired ten years ago."

Drake nodded. "Got it."

"Do you like coffee cake?"

"I don't think there's a thing on your menu I wouldn't like," he mumbled, eyes still on the board.

"Let me choose something for you."

"Please do." He jerked his gaze from the board to look Liz in the eyes again.

"Where ya from?" she asked as she turned away to fill a big red mug with regular drip coffee.

"Overland Park." He pulled his phone from his pocket and glanced at the screen. Two bars.

"Hmm." She studied his face for a moment as she slid the chunky mug over the counter.

"Hmm what?" Slowly, he lifted his chin to look at her. Putting his phone down, he picked up the mug.

"Figured you'd say Los Angeles or Phoenix."

"I wouldn't have a wool coat if I was from either of those places," he reminded her.

"Denver."

"Why?"

"Hang on." She held her hand up. "Let me get you something to eat."

"Thank you."

With another quick glance around the café, Drake took a sip of the hot coffee. Robust and strong, apparently unlike that at Dr. Vanderburg's office. The thought made him laugh. Was Dottie a little blue-haired lady who liked to knit scarves for holiday gifts?

An instrumental version of "Sleigh Ride" played from invisible speakers. Drake, who loved Christmas music from the Ratpack to trendy versions of the old classics and newer, indie songs to the silly kids' songs his brother and his wife played for his niece, appreciated the effort. The hidden speakers made it seem as if the music was piped in by magic.

Drake picked his phone up again and scrolled through his email. He'd had several drop in last night before the storm got bad. Nothing that couldn't wait, but the idea of not having good cell service while he was here made him a little twitchy. First up, he needed to contact his family, preferably his brother. Even better, his sister-in-law. She wouldn't make a big deal out of what had happened. His brother probably wouldn't, but now and then he and Andrew still acted like kids. Drake wouldn't put it past Andrew to tell his parents what had happened just to stir the pot.

"Here ya go."

Liz reappeared with what looked like a slice of coffee cake. The slice looked big enough it could easily be half the cake.

"I guessed Los Angeles and Phoenix thinking maybe you're not used to driving in snow."

Drake snorted softly, but he ducked his head when he felt the heat of embarrassment in his cheeks.

"Used to it, but apparently, not enough respect for it."

"You got a little big for your britches. Is that what you're saying?"

Liz's smile was warm; her eyes lined with crow's feet. Still, Drake thought she looked youngish, maybe his mom's age. Her blue eyes sparkled with happiness or maybe holiday spirit.

"Something like that, I guess." He picked up the fork she'd laid across the plate. "This looks delicious."

"Oh, it is." She nodded.

"Are you the baker?"

"I am."

The door opened, and a bell jingled to announce someone's arrival. Drake hadn't even noticed that when he had come in. He glanced over his shoulder to see the same person he'd nearly bumped into earlier on the sidewalk. With the bulky Carhartt coat and the black beanie pulled down low over her forehead, it had taken him a minute earlier to discern if it was a woman or man. He'd noticed the big gray snow boots, too, but again, still wasn't certain.

It had been her eyes when she'd looked at him that told him the figure dressed for snow was a woman. Black onyx shined, fringed in long, thick eyelashes. A peaches and cream complexion and the hint of hoop earrings under the beanie. Drake wondered what she looked like under the bulky work coat. He liked the way her skinny jeans fit her, but even that was hard to see well because of how the coat covered so much. From the look she'd given him on the sidewalk earlier, if she caught him looking too closely at her, especially at her butt, she might throat punch him.

"Kynlee." Liz smiled at the woman as she tugged the beanie off and walked across the room to stand at the counter next to Drake. "What's up, kid?"

Drake eyed Liz and turned to peek at the other woman, wondering what she would think of being called kid.

"Brock and Holly are having a snowball fight in their front yard." The woman rolled her eyes.

"Sounds like fun." Liz shrugged. "Drake, this is my daughter, Kynlee."

Daughter?

Stunned, Drake turned the stool sideways to get a better look. Maybe they had the same facial structure? Their lips were shaped the same, but there was something about Kynlee's that made him think kissing her would be a good idea. Something in her frown that warned him it most certainly wouldn't be a good idea.

"Kyn, this is Drake."

"You're the idiot who crossed the bridge and buried his SUV off Fifty-seven." Kynlee's eyebrows shot up in a challenge. "Right?"

"Kynlee." Liz sighed. Her tone was more resigned than sharp. "Would you learn some manners, please? Locals know you're prickly, but you could be nice to tourists."

"Tourists," Kynlee repeated, seemingly unfazed by what her mother had just said. "Right."

"Want coffee?"

"I do." Kynlee nodded. She unzipped her coat and slipped it off. Rather than hanging it up on the rack by the door, she slung it over the stool next to Drake and sat on it. The black t-shirt wasn't frilly, but it hugged her slender frame and accentuated her assets. A stack of bangle bracelets jangled on her right arm as she rested her hands on the counter.

"Did you just come to gripe about your sister?"

"That and to gossip about the idiot who drove over the bridge in a blizzard."

Drake laughed out loud when she turned those onyx eyes on him.

"But I made it over the bridge," he reminded her.

"Luck." She shrugged and turned to watch Liz pour her coffee.

"Forgive my daughter," Liz said to him. "I don't know where the attitude comes from, but it's always been there. In spades."

Even Kynlee snorted at Liz's comment.

"Is that coffee cake?" Kynlee pointed at his plate.

"Yep. Want some?"

Kynlee nodded. "I took donuts to the rec center earlier. A dozen. They wiped them out."

Donuts? To the rec center?

Seemed like a nice thing to do, if not outright festive. Drake finally took a bite of the coffee cake. He chewed it slowly, careful not to moan out loud at how rich, how sweet, it was.

"Dad's still out plowing driveways," Liz told her.

"I know. I did a few, but he told me he'd handle the rest. I thought maybe Brock was helping him."

"Hence your coming in to tattle." Liz gave Kynlee a look Drake assumed was the mom look. Her smile tempered the sternness of it, though.

"I mean, I thought we were adults." Kynlee picked up her mug and held it in front of her face with both hands.

"Everyone needs a little playtime, Kyn," Liz told her. "Be right back."

CHAPTER FOUR

"Not a big fan of snowball fights, huh?" The guy stared at her boldly while enjoying her mom's coffee cake.

"Not when there's work to be done," she answered, ignoring that nagging feeling in her gut. When had she *ever* been a big fan of snowball fights? She wasn't much for snow, which again, didn't go well with living in the Midwest. Could be worse. She could live in the Dakotas or Minnesota. But she could also have packed her life up and moved to Florida or Arizona, too. No snow there. She helped her dad with the landscaping, more so now that her mom had bought the café and reopened it. Odds were she could get a job in a warm state doing landscaping.

She would have to leave the girls, though. Kynlee didn't kid herself. While she had been an all-state basketball player when she was younger, she knew there were other people here in Reindeer Meadow just as qualified to coach the high school girls. Maybe even more so, because some of those people were teachers, too.

Kynlee would sooner throw snowballs at Santa while ice-skating than find herself teaching high school kids anything.

"What do you do?" the guy asked her.

She shook her head. He had already asked her one question; she would take a turn now.

"Why were you on the road last night?"

At her question, maybe at her frown, the guy—had her mom called him Drake?—sighed. He appeared to deflate right in front of her.

"Mm." She nodded. "Lemme guess. You were on your way home for a good old-fashioned Christmas with your family. Can't miss it. Can't even be late, or your mom will be upset with you."

"I have a meeting in Champaign."

Kynlee tipped her head and wrapped her hands around her mug just as her mom reappeared with a slice of coffee cake for her. Kynlee eyed her portion and compared it to Drake's.

"Why'd he get a bigger piece?" She picked up her fork and aimed a look at her mom. She was kidding, and her mom knew it, but the guy didn't.

"Hardly," he mumbled.

She laughed softly. "Must have been an important meeting."

Drake looked up with a grin. He shrugged. "Eh. Snow doesn't scare me. Obviously, I've never flipped my car before."

"We had a few inches of ice before the snow," she told him.

"So I gathered." He took another bite. "I just wanted to get into Illinois. Make the drive shorter today. So I could get the meeting wrapped up and get back home."

Kynlee quirked her eyebrows and nodded when he stopped talking. "To your good old-fashioned Christmas with your family."

"I'm sensing that you're not a fan of good old-fashioned Christmases with family, either."

"Maybe bonking your head knocked some sense into you after all."

"Your family doesn't celebrate Christmas?" Drake sounded like a six-year-old surprised to find out reindeer don't really fly.

"Oh, they do." She nodded and lifted her fork for a bite.

"But you don't?"

"Under protest," she answered. "I tried once to skip it. My sister had a freakin' cow."

"She's younger than you?"

"She's older, and at the time, she was twenty-two."

Drake laughed softly.

"Is this the sister involved in a snowball fight? When she should be working?"

"Technically, she's off today." Kynlee nodded. "She teaches second grade. So she's off for Christmas break. And if she wasn't, she would have a snow day."

"She's a teacher. And what do you do?"

Kynlee smiled when he asked the question again.

"I help my dad with the landscaping business," she answered simply. "And all kinds of odd jobs. I should be clearing driveways right now, but I assumed since Dad told me he had it covered that Brock was helping him."

Drake nodded as he took another bite of the cake. Kynlee stole a glance at him while he was looking at the chalkboard menu. He had thick brown hair, a bit longish, a bit messy, and yet, Kynlee could imagine it combed neatly. His warm brown eyes made her think of whiskey; his cheekbones were strong and sharp. A neat bit of scruff covered his face.

Definitely nice to look at.

Which was why she made herself look away.

"I coach the girls' basketball team, too."

"Yeah?" He looked at her with interest. "That's cool."

She stared at him for a moment, wondering if he was sincere.

"I can't hit a layup to save my life." His grin was a bit sheepish. "But I averaged five and a half yards per carry when I played football."

"College football?" That was impressive. The guy was built, but she figured next to an NFL running back or even a college Big Ten player he would look like a middleschool kid.

"No." He rolled his eyes. "High school."

"What do you do?" she asked him around another bite. "Besides make bad decisions about driving in bad weather?"

"I work in IT. Heading to a training meeting in Champaign."

"Training for you?"

"No. Training for medical staff there. New software."

"Mmm." She winced. "In my experience, new software, even software updates, suck."

"Which is why you need me."

Kynlee laughed out loud and then slapped her hand over her mouth. She hadn't found a man yet that she needed. This one being in IT wouldn't be any different. She had buckled down and gotten through college; she'd even kept a better than average GPA. But she wasn't academic. She didn't love technology. And she hated the thought of being bound to a desk or a computer.

Which made her the perfect person to work with her dad now that her mom was stepping back from the business. Kynlee was happiest outside, doing *something*. *Anything*.

"That was a generalization," Drake told her. Kynlee gave him the side-eye as she sipped from her mug again. He didn't seem offended by what was probably an offensive, downright rude, response. In fact, the way he was grinning, she had to assume he was amused.

"Mm-hmm." She nodded.

"You're tough," he told her, still smiling when she turned to look him in the eyes.

She had been called worse. But the smile on his face, in his eyes, told her he was teasing. Kynlee took her last bite, wiped her mouth with a napkin, and put her fork down on her plate.

"Duty calls," she announced as she slid off the stool and grabbed her coat.

"Plowing driveways?"

"If that's what needs doing."

"Want company?"

Kynlee, in the process of putting her coat on, froze and looked up at him.

"You wanna ride with me to plow snow?"

"Nothin' better to do," he answered with a shrug.

"You just want tips on how to drive in this crap."

He flashed that grin at her again. Kynlee sank her teeth into her lower lip. Champaign-bound Drake was good-looking. Possibly dangerous.

But Kynlee was fearless.

"Sure. Why not?"

CHAPTER FIVE

"How long's it going to take to get your car ready to go?"

Drake looked at Kynlee across the cab of her pickup. She had cranked the heat up when they climbed in, and by now, both of them had taken their coats off.

"You're kidding, right?"

Stopped at a sign, Kynlee turned her head to face him. "Do I look like I'm kidding?"

The severe frown she wore looked like she might never kid or tease or laugh. But he knew better. She had been a little rough around the edges back at Frosty's, but she had laughed a bit. At him. With him. Didn't matter to Drake; he liked the sound of it.

"You look like you haven't kidded near enough in your life."

She tipped her head to study him before looking away and easing her foot off the brake. In the enclosed space with her, Drake could smell what he assumed was her perfume. Something rich and heavy and totally not what he would have expected from a woman who wore a functional outdoor coat and heavy winter snow boots.

He liked it. In fact, if he was in the cab with her too long, he might be giddy with the scent.

"What does that mean?"

"Don't get defensive." He shook his head. "I just—"

"Not being defensive," she snapped.

Drake simply stared at her, waiting for her to look at him again. When she did, her face was set in stone. He arched his eyebrows, relieved when the stone cracked slightly, and a small smile tilted her lips.

"You're very serious."

"Is there something wrong with that?"

"No." He shrugged. "Not at all. But there's nothing wrong with cutting up now and then, too."

"And by cutting up, you mean laughing."

"Laughing. Having fun. Being silly."

"Hmm." She smacked her lips together. "What about your car?"

"It's still on the side of the highway," he answered. "Some guy picked me up last night—"

"Calvin Grady," she supplied the name.

"Right." He nodded, but he kept his laugh to himself. "Anyway, it's a good thing he stopped."

"You think?"

"It was cold. I couldn't even get out of the SUV without his help."

"Did you roll it?"

"No. But it's on the passenger side. Had to have a bit of help climbing up and out."

"Did you injure anything? Other than the gash on your head?"

"Well, apparently, my pride. There's a pretty local woman here who has made it very well known that she thinks I'm an idiot."

Even with her eyes on the road in front of her, Drake saw her brows jump in amusement.

"Bumps and bruises." He looked away, swept his gaze around the front of the truck, and out the passenger's window. "You have to admit it's pretty. My mom would love this."

"So does mine, but no, that doesn't mean I have to admit anything."

"You don't like snow?" He whipped his head around to look at her again. She didn't answer right away. Simply gave him a half-hearted shrug.

"It's okay, I guess," she finally mumbled.

"You just don't like it with Christmas."

"I don't like Christmas."

"Why not?"

Kynlee sighed and glanced at him. "I dunno. I just don't."

"Your sister always got more presents than you? No, wait. You were on the naughty list every year?"

That made her laugh. Drake relaxed a bit in his seat.

"I'm sure Holly and I were both on the naughty list plenty of years, but we always got presents. Santa always came."

"Someone jilted you. Left you at the altar on Christmas Eve?"

"No." She rolled her eyes. "Who says that? Jilted. That's like an outdated term."

"You lost a grandparent—"

"No." She raised her voice a bit and shrugged again. "No. I just don't care for Christmas."

"Hmm." He nodded, sensing it was time to back off. He couldn't help but study her, though. Her short dark hair left her ears exposed. The gold hoops in her ears appeared to be the real thing, not costume jewelry. Her profile was serious, all angles.

"What?" she asked a few moments later. Her laugh this time was one of discomfort. He was making her feel self-conscious.

"Nothing." He shook his head. "Sorry." Determined now not to stare at her, he looked out his window again. A line of woods ran parallel to the highway. Snowflakes still fell, though they appeared much less threatening now than they had the night before. The highway Kynlee drove had been cleared, but there was still a mess of slush and bits of ice on the ground.

"Why do you like Christmas?"

"What?"

"What is it about Christmas that you like?"

He glanced at her, surprised at her question. Even a bit intrigued by her question. How could she not understand the draw of Christmas? How did she not feel it?

"Family, I guess," he mumbled after thinking about it for a few seconds.

"But I'm close to my family. And family's not Christmas."

"No, but for me, Christmas is family."

"Explain."

At a loss for words, Drake hesitated. She sounded sincere. But if she was close to her family and still didn't equate family with Christmas, how could he explain the way he did?

"Years of memories," he finally started. "My brothers and I staying up late, waiting for Santa to come. Falling asleep in the living room and waking up in our bedrooms, excited but sad that we missed Santa again. My mom with the camera snapping pictures as we took in the tree and the presents. My Grandma's homemade stuffing, and my aunt's sugar cookies. Sled riding with my cousins."

She didn't speak when he stopped talking, but Drake noticed her grip on the steering wheel tighten. Finally, she slowed and hit the turn signal. They had cleared four drive-ways so far, all of them remote homes, off the beaten path. Kynlee's four-wheel-drive truck handled the country roads easily.

This place appeared to be a big, old farmhouse. In the daylight, there were no pretty Christmas lights, but Drake saw lights hanging from the eaves of the house. A giant snowman and Santa dominated the front yard. Drake watched Kynlee as she eyed the drive; she paid no attention at all to the yard decorations.

His phone buzzed in his coat pocket. He slipped it out and saw that it was a call from Allen Josephs in Champaign. He had put in a call to Allen first thing in the morning to let him know he wouldn't make the meeting unless there was a Christmas miracle. The last part had been a joke, of course. Drake wouldn't get to the meeting in Champaign today no matter what.

"Excuse me," he said quietly as he tapped the screen and put the phone to his ear. "Allen."

"Hey, Drake." His colleague and friend sounded concerned. "Just got your message, man. You okay?"

"Yeah, I'm fine. But my car's not."

"Beat up pretty badly?"

"No idea. Still off the highway where I left it last night."

"Ouch." Allen groaned. "Okay. We'll be fine here. I'll get you all the notes from the meeting. I think Gwen Hayward's still going to make it."

"Good."

Gwen was Drake's colleague, too. She worked for the same company, but she lived in Tennessee. Hopefully, she wouldn't have any issues with the drive. The snowstorm had come cross Kansas and Missouri.

"Take it easy, man. Have a Merry Christmas."

"Merry Christmas to you, too," he said before he hung up.

Kynlee was moving snow when he hung up. He hadn't even paid attention to how she maneuvered the truck while he was on the phone.

"I could say all the same things," she finally said after a few minutes of quiet, the only sound the tires on the snow-covered drive. "Santa came to see me and Holly. We left him cookies and milk. We went to my grandma's house every year."

"And that isn't Christmassy to you?"

"I don't want it to be," she said simply. "Why can't that be any day? Any Sunday afternoon?"

"It can be," he agreed. "But why can't Christmas be special?"

She shrugged, eyes on the rearview mirror.

"Is it that you don't believe? Like, the nativity and stuff?"

Kynlee glanced at him, her depthless eyes swallowing him whole.

"I do believe that," she said quietly. "I do. I go to church on Christmas. I just don't love the commercial side of it."

"Hmm." He nodded. "Okay."

"I mean, Holly and I were spoiled. But do you know how many kids don't get presents for Christmas? How many kids don't have breakfast or lunch every day let alone a big turkey dinner on Christmas day?"

"I do," he said quietly.

"And yet, you still love Christmas."

With a scowl on her face, she looked back at the windshield and focused her attention on the snow and the plow on the front of the truck.

CHAPTER SIX

KYNLEE PUNCHED THE RADIO POWER BUTTON AFTER THEIR SILENCE grew too big for the cab of her truck. Wondering if she had made him mad with her Christmas ranting, she stole glances at him as she drove. One more house to worry about for now. According to her dad's text, they were nearly done with their regular customers. Didn't mean anything. Kynlee would spend the day helping anyone who needed it. But she would finish the Peter's house and then check in with her dad before doing anything else.

Maybe she needed to deliver Mr. Christmas back to Frosty's café. He probably preferred her mom's company to hers.

The country station she usually listened to was playing a George Strait Christmas song. With a sigh, she tapped the screen to change the station. Mariah Carey's big Christmas song. Another tap brought "I Want a Hippopotamus for Christmas" up.

She groaned and shot Drake a look when he laughed.

"Maybe it's because I was born here, you know," she said thoughtfully.

"Here," he repeated. "Like here. In Reindeer Meadow, Illinois?"

"Yep." She nodded.

"What do you mean?"

"Don't tell me you haven't heard the folklore about Reindeer Meadow?"

When he didn't answer her, Kynlee looked at him again. But he only shook his head.

"I figured it was something to do with the number of deer in the area. Deer hunting's big here, isn't it?"

"It is," she agreed, "but no, that's not it."

"Enlighten me."

She smiled in spite of herself. "Legend has it that the Fayrweather Christmas Tree Farm here in Reindeer Meadow is a place where magic happens."

"What? Like, a family goes out looking at trees and when they find the one meant for them, the tree lights up or something?"

Kynlee laughed softly.

"No. So, Elmer and Lydia Fayrweather settled Reindeer Meadow. Back in the 1800s. Elmer was from Ireland, Lydia from Germany. I don't know why they chose the area, especially with it being right on the Mississippi."

"Has it flooded before?"

"Yeah." Kynlee nodded. "The whole town went under in the Big Flood of '93. Could have just wiped it off the map, but people wanted to rebuild."

"That's why so many buildings look new."

"New and mostly that prefabricated style. Lots of trailers, too."

"And so how is the tree farm magic?"

"That I'm not sure of," she answered. "Elmer and Lydia had nine kids. One son took over the farm. That son and his wife had eleven kids. One son took over the farm. And on and on."

"Okay." He nodded.

"It's actually..." She sighed.

"What?"

"I can't believe I'm saying this, but it's a nice place. Fun, I guess, for kids to visit."

"Ooh." Drake grinned and waggled his eyebrows. "Careful, there. You sound a little Christmassy."

She laughed and rolled her eyes.

"So, from the beginning of the farm, of the town, the Fayr-weathers have been good, strong community people. They pitch in. They do whatever it takes to get anything needed done. They sandbag if the river rises. They donate money to the schools and to the nursing home. They sponsor blood drives. They're good people."

"Sounds like it."

"Well, legend says that if you wish for love, and you're pure in heart, take the one you love to the tree farm."

"And that's it? You get your love? So, it's like a love potion? Or Cupid's arrow?"

"Yeah, but you have to be pure in heart."

"And do you know any couples who fell in love at the tree farm?"

She squirmed in her seat and avoided his intense gaze. "I do. But I don't believe their relationships exist only because of the tree farm. I mean, they had to be in love before they were there, right? And the tree farm is magical, and maybe then they confess their feelings."

"How do you feel about love, Kynlee who doesn't like Christmas?"

She chewed on her lip when she wanted to smile.

"Been there, done that. But never the forever kind, I guess."

"Have you been to the tree farm?" Drake tipped his head and narrowed his eyes at her.

"No." She snorted. "Not since I was maybe ten. And we went as a family."

"Did your parents meet there?"

"No. They went to college together in Missouri."

"Hmm." He nodded. "That's interesting."

"My parents?"

"No. The legend of Reindeer Meadow."

"I guess to me Christmas should be...a more personal... thing? If you have faith in God and stuff. It shouldn't be commercial. And as far as loving a family and spending time together, I think it's wrong to have one day for that. Same with Valentine's Day. Family is an everyday thing, not something you clamor for to get together and have fun with once a year. Valentine's Day implies you don't have to treat the one you love special every day of the year."

She glanced at him when she felt his heavy gaze on her. But Drake said nothing. Simply tssked and turned away from her.

"What?" she finally asked when he still didn't say anything after a few moments.

"Well, I mean, I agree. Family is every day. Being too busy for one another every day and suddenly dropping everything to be together that one day is maybe hypocritical. On the other hand, don't you think most families are like that? Close? You said your family is."

"We are."

"And maybe, I mean, Kynlee, there are a lot of families, a lot of friends, even, spread across the country. The globe, even. And what's wrong with those people making the extra effort at this time of year to get together and catch up?"

He had a point, but Kynlee wasn't one to give in that easily. Still, wouldn't she sound like a horrible person if she said it was wrong for people to spend time together?

"What about people who work forty or fifty hours a week? What if your sister lived in Idaho and worked every day and only got four days off in December? Wouldn't you want her to come home those four days in December?"

"Why Idaho?"

Drake laughed and tossed his hands up in defeat. "Go with me here, Kynlee."

With an exasperated sigh, she finally nodded. "Yeah, I guess so."

From the corner of her eye, she saw him nod.

"What was that?"

"What?" He shook his head.

"I saw that. You nodded. Like you were addressing a jury. You just said *I rest my case*."

"Did not."

"You did. In your head. You said it."

"Okay, maybe, but you have to admit. I just scored a point in the pro-Christmas column."

"But there's still no need for Santa and presents and the goofy songs." She waved her hand at the radio, now playing "Grandma Got Run Over by a Reindeer."

"Do you listen to regular music?"

"Of course."

"Well, then, I absolutely disagree. Christmas music has a place during the Christmas season."

"Which is not pre-Halloween."

"No, it's not, I agree."

39

Close to the turn off for Emmet Peter's house, Kynlee slowed again and made a right when she came to the snow-covered gravel road.

"You just like to argue, don't you?"

Kynlee burst out laughing and glanced at him.

"I do, yes. You sound just like my sister."

"I might need to meet your sister."

"She's married." Kynlee shook her head.

"To Brock, I'm assuming. But I said meet her, not date her."

"Tell me about your brothers."

"One is married with a little girl. The other is younger than me, uglier than me, and a total pain in the ass."

"Wow." She nodded, eyes wide as she leaned forward to navigate the snow. Since no one had been out here yet, it was a bit tricky to know where the road ended, and the usual grassland started. "Okay, then."

"You asked," he reminded her.

Her phone buzzed. Not wanting to take her eyes off the windshield, the winter wonderland in front of the truck, Kynlee tossed it to Drake.

"Read that for me."

"Passcode?"

"Hmm." She cleared her throat. "Zero nine one three one seven."

He tapped the number in and then chuckled.

"What?" She hunched her shoulders, wondering if she made a mistake asking him to check her text messages.

"It's from your mom. And it says bring that hot guy home for dinner tonight."

"OhmyGod." She snorted and shook her head. She wouldn't put it past her mother to say such a thing. But she was praying Drake was kidding. "Seriously?"

"Well, okay, no. She said bring Drake home with you for dinner tonight."

Kynlee shot him a glance as the heavy brush and skeletal trees opened to reveal the sprawling brick ranch home in front of them.

"That's not a prefab home," Drake whistled his appreciation.

"It's not," she agreed.

"Thanks for letting me come with you," he said apropos of nothing.

"Nothing better to do, right?"

"You're fun," he said simply. "But I could have been a serial killer. I might have crashed my car on purpose."

"I don't scare easily, Drake," she told him. "And if you tried to kill me, I would've just shoved you out the passenger door and left you to freeze in the snow."

"Ouch."

"Truth hurts."

"So does frostbite, as I'm told."

"Just mind your p's and q's."

"Are you taking me home for dinner?"

"Do you wanna come for dinner?"

"I would love that," he answered. He sounded sincere, but Kynlee noticed a dark look come over his face.

"What? Mom's a good cook."

He laughed softly. "I haven't told my family what happened."

"Ah." She snorted and shook her head. "Good luck with that, man. Bet you catch some hell."

"You have no idea."

CHAPTER SEVEN

THE AUSTIN HOUSE LOOKED A LOT LIKE THE LAST HOUSE KYNLEE had driven to earlier. Sprawling brick, floor to ceiling windows in the family room, and a chimney that reached upward to the clouds, which were still spitting bits of snow. As dusk had fallen around the small town, Christmas lights had begun to pop on everywhere. Drake had seen some lights last night, but he had been a little too shaken to pay much attention.

Now, though, he looked his fill. When Kynlee finished moving snow, she had given him a ride back into the small-town square. He'd spent the previous night in the home of someone named Cecil, but the only person he had seen there was a woman. Older with silver hair and a bit of a plump belly, Drake had mentally compared her to Mrs. Claus. He wondered what Kynlee would think of that.

Kynlee had let him out of the truck on the square and told him she would be back to get him around five. She was gone before he could tell her where he was staying, but he decided she already knew. He had no idea what she did when she dropped him off, but he wandered the square with his coat buttoned to his chin and his gloved hands tucked in his pockets.

Red garland adorned every light post on the square. Silver bells hung on every corner, either from stoplights or from street signs. Christmas music had played around the square as he walked; the old-fashioned kind one would hear in old Irving Berlin movies. Drake couldn't imagine living in a small town like this during the holidays and not eating it up. His parents would like Reindeer Meadow, especially his mom. He wished he could share it with her.

To that end, he took a few pictures on his phone as he wandered the square. He captured the garland and silver bells, but he also took pictures of a few store windows decked out for the holiday. There was a giant Christmas tree on the lawn in the square. Drake could see there were lights on it, but they weren't lit until nearly five when he headed back to Cecil's to freshen up in time for Kynlee to come and get him.

Once in his small but neat room, he took his coat off for a while and sat in the blue accent chair in the corner. A tiny white ceramic tree with blue lights was the only holiday decoration in the room, but he liked it. Anything bigger would have been too much. He called his parents and left a minimal message about a little trouble on the roads and not making it to his meeting in Champaign. Hung up after a promise that he was fine, and he would be in touch about getting home for Christmas.

It wouldn't appease his mom, but it was enough until later. When she called him and lit into him about driving in the blizzard. Crossing the bridge. Losing control and flipping

44

his SUV. Kynlee had picked him up at five on the dot. They hadn't exchanged numbers, and she didn't come to the door. Maybe she was afraid Cecil would think she was there to pick him up for a date. Instead, she pulled to the curb in front of Cecil's two-story bungalow and tapped her horn.

They had talked on the eight-minute drive to Kynlee's parents' house.

Not about Christmas. Or any holiday. Kynlee had seemed troubled when he climbed into her truck, and he asked what was wrong. She had been skittish to share, but eventually, she told him she was concerned about one of her ball players. Not a good home life, and most likely made worse by the snowstorm. Both in keeping her parents at the house all day and in keeping everyone tense and stir-crazy inside.

Drake glanced at her as she steered the truck down the long drive to the house. The Austin's house was lit up like something he would expect to see in a Christmas movie. Simple gold lights dotted the eaves, the dormer windows, along the entire front and sides of the house. The same lights outlined a massive front door and the bushes and hedges out front. A manger scene decorated the yard, complete with a glowing golden star rigged above it with some kind of wire.

Drake loved it. He couldn't wait to see the interior of the house. The Christmas tree.

But even more, he loved the way the tension on Kynlee's face eased as she watched the house grow closer and closer. She wasn't smiling, but the lines around her eyes faded. Her forehead smoothed as the frown eased.

Maybe she just liked being at her parents' house.

But maybe she liked the Christmas lights and didn't want to admit it.

Maybe she didn't even realize the effect they had on her.

"Where do Holly and Brock live?" he asked her as they made their way up the front walk.

"In town. About two blocks south of the square."

Drake eyed the two trucks in the driveway and glanced at her.

"Yeah, the white one is Dad's. The silver one is Brock's."

So, he was going to meet the whole family. Drake didn't mind. In fact, he was looking forward to it.

"Listen." She cleared her throat when they stood together on the wide, wrap-around porch.

"Look, if there's mistletoe hanging there, just blast on through. Not a big deal."

She laughed and shook her head.

"Or, anywhere in the house. I won't kiss you. It's cool."

"Why wouldn't you?" She tipped her head and shrugged.

"Why wouldn't I—?"

"Kiss me." She licked her lips, drawing Drake's attention to them. Perfectly pink. Smiling just slightly now. "I mean, you're Mr. Christmas. You love all things Christmas. But if there's mistletoe, you don't wanna kiss me?"

Drake very much wanted to kiss her, but with all her mixed signals, he wouldn't be surprised if he kissed her, and she punched him in the nose.

"Oh." She nodded. "Oh, God. Okay. Yeah."

"What in the world was that all about?" He was starting to shiver, ready to get inside and warm up. But the smug look on her face, the tone of her voice, made him curious. Drake would stand outside and freeze his nuts off to find out what she was thinking.

"You're married."

He held his hands in front of him and shook his head. "Nope."

"Not all married people wear rings."

"Not married."

"But involved—"

"No. Not married. Not engaged. Not dating anyone."

"Mmm." She sighed. Nodded as she turned to the door. Drake didn't like that little noise any more than her previous comment.

"What?" He lunged for her, hooked his fingers in the bend of her elbow before she could open the door. "What does that mean?"

"You just don't want to." She shrugged. "Not a big deal."

"You think I—?" He groaned out loud. "That I don't—?" Fingers still curled around her arm, Drake decided the only way to clear up this misunderstanding was to kiss her. He hauled her closer, but as he leaned toward her the door opened. Heat and Bing Crosby's voice and a golden retriever all roared out of the house at them.

Drake blinked and looked at the door with dread, expecting to see Liz watching them. Or worse—Kynlee's dad.

Instead, she found himself looking at a slightly different version of Kynlee. Shorter. Somewhat curvier. Longer hair of the same color that fell over her shoulders in waves. Her face was shaped like a heart, her eyes holly green, rather than the bottomless black of Kynlee's.

This had to be Holly. Cute, yes. By Kynlee's own admission, maybe nicer and easier to talk to. But Drake's gaze was drawn back to the woman standing nearly toe-to-toe with him.

"What are you guys doing out here?" Holly's voice was loud enough that people on the square in town could probably hear her. Most definitely Kynlee's parents.

"Hey, Max." Kynlee ignored her sister and greeted the dog instead. "How's my buddy?"

"C'mon." Holly nodded her head to the living room. "Dinner's about ready."

Wishing he would have had a few more minutes alone with Kynlee, Drake dropped his arm to his side and followed her into the house.

"Holly, this is Drake." She gestured to him as she unzipped her coat. "I didn't get your last name."

"Palmer."

"Drake Palmer." She shrugged out of her coat, dropped it to the floor, and leaned over to tug her boots off. "Drake, my sister Holly."

"Nice to meet you," Holly said sincerely. He shook her hand and then went to work on the buttons of his coat. "Wanna beer?"

Drake opened his mouth to answer, unsure what to say. A beer sounded good, but he didn't want to be the only person at dinner drinking one.

"I'm betting he does."

He looked up as the man who had to be Kynlee and Holly's dad crossed the open living space with two longneck bottles in hand.

"And if he doesn't, he will when he hears the news."

"What news?" Kynlee asked as she moved sock-footed to a closet and hung her coat up. She held her hand out to take Drake's, eyes still on her dad.

"Lester wrecked the tow truck about an hour ago," he answered. "You're not gonna get that vehicle of yours outta the snow anytime soon."

CHAPTER EIGHT

"Whoa boy." Kynlee winced. "I'm sorry."

Drake sighed and shrugged as he took the bottle her dad offered.

"Not much I can do about it," he answered. "Thank you, Sir."

"Daniel," the man told him.

"Drake." He shook Daniel's hand before taking a drink. The beer was so cold, Drake would believe it if Daniel told him they kept bottles buried out in the snow.

"Where's Brock?" Kynlee asked Holly.

"Helping Mom."

Drake wondered what Liz was making. It smelled delicious, and he was hungry. He had skipped lunch, though at the time it hadn't bothered him. He'd been enjoying himself riding along with Kynlee.

"Dinner's ready!" Liz called.

Daniel and Holly headed to the big table at the far wall of the room. Floor to ceiling glass here provided a good view of a wooded area out back. Christmas lights glowed at the top of the house and reflected a bit in the snow on the ground. Inside, in the corner of the big open room, the Austin's Christmas tree held court. Drake guessed it must be twelve foot tall. Decorated in all shapes and colors of ornaments, it was both festive and cozy.

Drake glanced again at Kynlee wondering how she wasn't caught up in the Christmas spirit.

"Hey, Drake."

"Hi, Liz." He offered the woman a smile. "Thank you so much for inviting me to dinner."

"You're welcome, of course." She patted his arm. "Chili or homemade vegetable soup. And the bread's homemade, too."

Drake's stomach rumbled.

"Please." Kynlee nodded at the crockpots on the island counter. "Help yourself."

Feeling a bit funny about being the first to serve himself, Drake looked at the bottle in his hand. Kynlee held her hand out and took it when he passed it to her.

"Brock Sanderson."

Drake nodded at the tall blond guy as he filled his bowl with thick, chunky vegetable soup. His stomach rumbled again, but no one seemed to hear it.

"Drake Palmer."

He took a slice of warm bread and slathered butter over it before moving toward the table. Not sure where to sit he glanced at Kynlee. She made her way across the room and put his beer down at a spot.

"You can sit by me, since you've learned I don't bite."

Drake laughed softly as he put his bowl and saucer on the table. Would she have bitten if he had kissed her out there on the porch? A little too intrigued by the thought, he forced himself to focus on the steaming soup and how hungry he was. Brock joined him at the table within seconds, pulling out the chair across from him without hesitation.

"Traveling for business, huh?"

Drake nodded at Brock. "I was, yeah. Now I guess I'll be hanging around here and waiting on my car."

"I can't believe Lester wrecked the tow truck." Brock dipped his spoon in his bowl of chili.

"What happened?"

"Lost control of it on the highway and rear ended someone already off the road."

"Do you guys get this severe weather often?"

"Once or twice a year, maybe," Brock answered. "Usually, we get hit a time or two with an ice storm. Or a snowstorm. Just your luck you were driving through both."

"Least he made it over the bridge," Kynlee said as she put her bowl at the place setting beside his. He tipped his head up, waiting for her to calling him an idiot again. But she only shot him a cute little smirk as she sat down beside him.

"How bad's your vehicle?" Daniel asked as he joined them at the table.

"No idea." Drake shrugged. "Guessing there's some pretty creases in the passenger side. Slid quite a way after flipping."

"How many stitches?" Holly asked with a nod in his direction. Drake resisted the urge to touch the bandage on his head.

"Four," he answered with a shrug. "Not a big deal."

"Talk to your parents yet?"

Drake narrowed his eyes at Kynlee. "I called and got voicemail."

"Your family doesn't know what happened?" Liz asked him. Still standing by the counter, she watched him as Holly finished dishing up her dinner.

"Well, no. Not exactly. I did call and leave a message."

"That you went off the road in a snowstorm?" Kynlee asked sweetly.

"Just told them I had an issue on the road and wasn't going to make it to my meeting in Champaign."

"You lied? To your parents?" Liz gaped at him.

"Withholding information is not the same as lying," Kynlee told her mom.

"It most certainly is, Kynlee. It's dishonest."

"But maybe better to be a little dishonest in a voicemail of that nature," Daniel suggested.

"A little dishonest," Liz mumbled to herself as she finally filled her own bowl. "That's like being a little pregnant, isn't it?"

Drake happened to catch the look Holly and Brock shared, as if they had a secret. No way he was going to call them on it. He didn't know them, and any secrets they had weren't his business.

"What?"

Apparently, Kynlee saw the look, too.

"What?" Holly shrugged. She nibbled on a bite of bread.

"Who won the snowball fight?"

Holly's face lit up as she glanced from Kynlee to Brock. "I did."

"Whatever." Brock rolled his eyes.

"You should have joined us. Imagine two against one," Holly said with a wink at Kynlee. "Brock wouldn't stand a chance."

Drake glanced at Kynlee to see her watching her sister with a thoughtful expression.

"We have something to tell you," Holly announced, turning her attention to encompass the whole table now. From the corner of his eye, Drake saw Daniel wrap his fingers around his bottle. Liz simply stilled in her seat and watched Holly. Drake wasn't sure she was breathing.

Kynlee's face had transformed. She wasn't grinning; in fact, her lips were barely tipped upward. But her face looked lighter again, the frown lines in her forehead long gone. She watched Holly closely.

"We are going to have a baby," Holly said with a small smile. She reached blindly over the table and laced her fingers with Brock's.

"A baby?" Liz breathed the words, clearly in awe of the idea.

"I'm going to be an aunt?" Kynlee asked, finally breaking into a big smile.

"A baby." Holly nodded. "You're going to be an aunt. And you're going to be grandparents."

Holly met Drake's eyes and chuckled softly. "And you're going to go home and tell your family about the weird Austin family you met, who announced a new baby coming when you just happened to be over for dinner."

"Not weird," he argued. "Congratulations."

"Thank you." Holly and Brock spoke at the same time.

"Oh my God!" Kynlee, as if Drake's word spurred her into action, jumped up from her seat. "A baby! You're gonna be a mom, Hol!"

Holly climbed to her feet and threw her arms around Kynlee. Drake and his brothers didn't do a lot of hugging, but this was the family dynamic he was used to. High emotions and sharing news—big and little—over dinner conversations.

This was the family dynamic that seemed to him to go hand in hand with that warm, festive holiday feeling. It made him a little sad for Kynlee that she didn't feel it.

CHAPTER NINE

"When are you due?" their mom asked. Holly pulled away from Kynlee and hurried around the table to hug their mom.

"August."

"Congratulations." Dad pumped Brock's hand with a big smile on his face. Kynlee glanced at Drake, expecting him to look a little out of place. But he simply drank it all in with a warm, happy smile on his face.

"Do you have nieces or nephews?" she asked after throwing her arms around her brother-in-law for a quick hug. Kynlee slid onto her chair with one knee tucked up under her, turned to face Drake.

"One niece," he answered. "She's two."

Kyle touched Drake's arm. "What's her name?"

"Addison. She's my older brother's daughter. Adorable."

"Pictures?"

Drake nodded and pulled his phone from his pocket.

"Let him eat while his soup is hot, Kyn." Her mom shook her head at her like she was ten years old again, begging her dad to go outside and shoot baskets with her.

"It's not problem," Drake assured them as he handed his phone over to Kynlee. A bright-eyed redhead beamed at her from the screen.

"She's a doll." Kynlee laughed.

"She is," he agreed. When Kynlee gave him his phone back, he dutifully passed it on to her mom. The guy didn't seem to mind that her whole family passed his phone around the table to check out his niece.

"Do you know what you're having?" he asked looking first at Holly and then Brock.

"We don't want to know," Brock answered.

Kynlee aimed a no-nonsense look at Holly. "Really? You? You don't want to know, Miss Nosy Pants?"

Holly laughed and shrugged. "Brock wants to be surprised, so I can wait, too."

"Mm-hmm." Kynlee picked up her spoon again and nodded. "We'll see how long that lasts."

"Hey!" Holly kicked her under the table. "I can be patient."

"What do you want?" Daniel asked the two of them.

"Twins," Brock said simply.

"Oh man." Kynlee flinched. "If you were my husband and you said that out loud, you'd be sleeping outside tonight, Brock."

"I just want a healthy baby," Holly answered.

"Goes without saying," Kynlee mumbled and waved her hand in a circle. "But if you could choose, would you have a boy or girl?"

"Boy."

"Girl."

Kynlee smirked at her sister and her husband. "Well, I guess if you had twins, you would have a chance at one of each."

"If you lived at my house, you'd be sleeping outside tonight." Holly pointed her spoon at Kynlee.

Conversation flowed as they finished their soups. They talked about the baby. About the holidays, though Kynlee didn't have much to add on that topic. And the likelihood of Drake getting home for Christmas.

"You could rent a car," her dad suggested.

Kynlee held her breath for a moment. Why did she hate that idea? She'd just met this guy this morning. But if she were being honest, she would have to admit she liked the idea of having him around for a while.

"You could." She pressed her lips together. "I could drive you into Hannibal. You could rent something and get home for Christmas."

Drake huffed out a tired sigh and shrugged. "Maybe. I guess I'll wait and see what things look like in the morning."

"Come over for breakfast," Kynlee's mom told him. "I'll set you up with a good cup of coffee and plenty to eat. That way if you decide to rent a car, you'll be ready to get on the road."

"You've done plenty for me already, Liz."

"Nonsense." Her mom shook her head. "It's no trouble."

"Do you think they'd have anything to rent right now?" Brock asked with a frown. "With it being three days before Christmas?"

"Can't hurt to check." Daniel shrugged.

When they finished dinner, her mom tried to shoo them all out of the kitchen. But Kynlee insisted she relax.

"Go talk about baby stuff." She waved her mom and sister away from the table as she stacked the bowls.

"Are you sure?"

"I'll help," Drake announced.

"You're a guest," Kynlee argued.

"Nope. I got to hear the family announcement," he reminded her. "So I can put some time in on clean up."

She laughed and shrugged. "Suit yourself."

Her parents and Holly and Brock settled into comfortable chairs in the living area; Liz and Holly talking at once about the baby.

"I don't expect you to help me," Kynlee told Drake as he stepped up at the sink beside her.

"My mother would never forgive me if I didn't help you."

Kynlee eyed his face as she rinsed the bowls and handed them to him.

"What?"

He took care with each bowl he put in the dishwasher.

"Your mom. She sounds interesting." She shrugged and leaned a bit sideways to turn toward him. "I'd like to meet her."

"You could drive me all the way home."

They shared a laugh.

"I will drive you into Hannibal tomorrow. If you want."

Drake nodded, but he didn't seem that concerned about getting home at the moment.

A loud roar of laughter went up from the living area behind them. Drake looked over his shoulder and then back at her.

"What're they doing?"

"Playing a new card game they're into now."

"Must be fun."

"It's crazy," she agreed.

"Kyn!"

Kynlee turned when Holly called her name.

"Are your girls doing anything tomorrow night?"

"They are," she answered with a nod. "But I've been sworn to secrecy."

"What's tomorrow night?" Drake asked her.

"Reindeer Meadow Christmas Festival." She finished rinsing the bowls and then started working on putting away leftovers.

"And what exactly happens at the Reindeer Meadow Christmas Festival?"

"What doesn't?" She glanced at him and rolled her eyes. "There's stuff in the square. Homemade candy and cookie booths. Hot chocolate. You can even go into Wonderland and get a beer or wine and have it out on the square."

"What's Wonderland?"

"The bar on the square."

Drake chuckled.

"It's enough to make me gag sometimes."

"What else happens?"

"There's ice skating."

"Really? Where?"

"Just a little man-made rink a couple of blocks south of the square. Do you ice skate?"

"Never tried it. You?"

"Used to, but I gave it up when I was in high school."

"Because of basketball."

She smiled and nodded.

"Kids sing. Actually, it's sort of a little talent show."

"And that's what your girls are doing?"

She mimed zipping her lips shut and tossing a key over her shoulder.

"And is this festival just for locals?"

"It's mostly locals that are there." She tipped her head and arched an eyebrow. "Because it's mostly locals that are here. We don't draw a lot of out-of-towners."

"From what I've seen of Reindeer Meadow, you should."

"But..." She shrugged. "If there were an out-of-towner in the area tomorrow night, he or she would be welcome to attend."

The way he smiled did something to her. Made her heart beat a little harder, a little quicker. Fingers a little shaky, she cleared her throat and dunked the interior bowl of one crockpot in the sink she'd filled with hot, soapy water.

"Do I need a date?"

Did he sound hopeful?

Kynlee reminded herself flirting with him was equivalent to flirting with trouble. Nothing that started between them could go anywhere, not with him living in Overland Park and her here in Reindeer Meadow.

"Is there mistletoe anywhere?"

She dropped her head back to cackle out loud.

CHAPTER TEN

"There's no mistletoe in the house." She glanced at him as she led him down the basement stairs. Admiring her backside just a second ago, Drake was relieved she hadn't caught him. He looked around now, noticing the garland and the lights on nearly everything a person could put garland and lights on. It was all tastefully done, but with so many Christmas decorations, the lack of mistletoe interested him.

"I'm not worried about mistletoe," he told her as she flipped a switch. Fluorescent lights shined from a drop-ceiling. Another Christmas tree, this one skinny, was tucked away in the far corner of the open family room.

"You were earlier."

"I thought you were," he answered.

"Hmm." She eyed him silently for a moment and finally turned away from him. "You play?"

Drake looked from her to the foosball table.

"Sure."

"I'm pretty good."

"I'm sure you are." He laughed. "But I was a champ back in college."

"And how long ago was that?"

"About twelve years ago."

"Me, too." She quirked an eyebrow at him as he approached the table. "We should play doubles."

"We'll get to that," she agreed. "First just us."

"I am curious," he said with another look around.

"About?" She squatted down and then popped up again with three balls in her hand.

"Why no mistletoe."

He wouldn't swear to it, but it looked like she blushed. She ducked her head quickly, though, and laughed for a moment.

"Well, we did have some once," she finally told him. "But Dad caught Holly trying to feed it to our dog. When we were little."

"What?"

"She thought it was spinach."

She looked up and met his eyes, still laughing. But two little red dimes sat on her cheeks, the tell-tale signs of embarrassment.

"I don't believe you."

"She did do that." She shrugged and looked down at the table.

"But?"

"But also, Dad may have caught me and a boyfriend making out down here. Under the mistletoe."

"How old were you?"

"Fourteen."

"And you were making out?" he yelped.

"Ssh!" She laughed and glanced at the stairs. "We were kissing. Lots of tongue."

"So you do like mistletoe." He drummed his fingers on the table. "Interesting."

"I was fourteen!" she reminded him and waved her hand at the table. "And...no. I didn't particularly like it."

"Much too young to be kissing with lots of tongue." He nodded.

"He was sixteen. I had to keep up with him."

"No wonder your dad banished the mistletoe." Drake stared at her with wide eyes. "Fourteen?"

"Are we playing?" she asked with a grin.

"Bring it." He nodded.

She beat him the first game. He beat her the second. Apparently, they were too loud, as by the time they were ready for the playoff game, Holly and Brock wandered downstairs to join them.

"I get the winner," Holly announced as she tucked her hands in her hip pockets, eyes on the table.

"You're pregnant," Kynlee reminded her.

"Yep. Playing for two."

"You ready?" Kynlee eyed Drake, a daring smile on her face.

"I think we should make this one interesting."

"Like what?"

"A little wager."

Kynlee nodded. "Okay. What's the bet?"

"If I win, you're my date for the Christmas festival tomorrow night."

Kynlee licked her lips and narrowed her eyes. "And if I win?"

"I don't know. What do you want?" he shrugged.

"Maybe don't answer that," Holly mumbled as she watched the two of them bantering.

Kynlee snorted.

"If I win, you have to buy me dinner before the Christmas festival."

"Deal." He nodded.

"Lame." Holly huffed and rolled her eyes.

"Go away." Kynlee waved her hand at her.

"Hol," Brock called to her from the tree. "We need to get an ornament for the baby."

"Not until next year."

"No, I mean one for you. Like expecting mother."

Drake watched Holly mosey over to stand with Brock at the tree.

"Ready now?"

"Yep." He nodded to Kynlee.

She dropped the ball through the hole, and Drake lined up his rod to take a kick. Before long, they were yelling and laughing, both spinning the bars insanely and ignoring the rules.

"Who's winning?" Holly hollered after several minutes of play.

"He is. By one."

"How bad do you want to eat tomorrow?" Holly asked Kynlee.

All of them were laughing as Drake dropped a ball into play. Kynlee lined her guy up to whack the ball straight at the goal. Drake jumped to the end of the table to block her shot. Arms flew as they both spun the rods, but finally, Kynlee put the ball in.

"That's a tie."

"We could always play one more point," Kynlee suggested.

"Or we could say you both won." Holly rested her hands on the table and leaned over it. "You could go to dinner, and then you could go to the Christmas Festival."

"And then you could play?" Kynlee quirked an eyebrow at her.

"Yes!"

"And you think she's gonna be able to wait nine months to see what you're having?" Kynlee looked at Brock over Holly's shoulder.

"Hey!" Holly leaned into Brock when he stepped closer. "Not fair."

"You can play Kynlee," Drake offered. "You be me. Play that final point."

Holly sidled up to take his place. "But do you want to win or lose?"

"If I get to be with your sister either way, I can't lose, can I?"

Holly shot Kynlee a look and waggled her eyebrows at her.

"Too bad Dad caught you with Brad Young and got rid of the mistletoe."

"Stop. It!" Kynlee laughed and shook her head.

"They have some at the store," Brock told them. "Just sayin'."

Drake met Kynlee's eyes, hoping she knew that if he wanted to kiss her, he had no plans to wait for mistletoe to appear.

CHAPTER ELEVEN

"KYNLEE, REMEMBER THE YEAR THE LADIES CLUB WAS OUT caroling and ended up at Wonderland shooting pool?"

Kynlee flicked her gaze up to meet Holly's eyes. Her sister dropped the ball through the game table chute when Kynlee laughed.

"I do remember that," she said with a nod. "But no, you didn't distract me." She grabbed the rod with a player closest to the ball and gave it a spin.

"Wait." Drake spoke from the end of the foosball table. "Someone here actually goes Christmas caroling?"

"Why would that surprise you?" Kynlee looked at him with a frown.

"Score!" Holly threw her fist in the air as Kynlee glanced at the table in time to see the ball roll past her goalie. "Drake wins."

"That was your fault." Kynlee pointed her finger at him.

"Still get you to be my date tomorrow night." He shrugged. "Tell me about the Christmas caroling."

"We should do that." Holly quirked an eyebrow at Kynlee.

"No."

"I'd do it," Drake announced. "But I wanna hear about the ladies club."

Holly snickered.

"There's a club that gets together monthly to play cards. Sometimes they have a special dinner event. They're kind of the welcome wagon when people move to Reindeer Meadow."

"Does that happen often?"

Kynlee snorted at Drake's question.

"No." Holly grinned. "Anyway, there's always a group of them who go caroling. Was it two years ago? They ended up in Wonderland shooting pool."

"So, it's not like all grandmas or anything, but there are a few older ladies in the group. I heard they closed the place down that night."

Holly nodded at Kynlee. "They were drinking cheap wine. Playing eight ball and snooker."

Drake looked surprised. He glanced at Brock. "I don't even know how to play snooker."

"Me neither." Brock shrugged.

"So, when they play cards, do they play poker?"

"Who knows?" Kynlee laughed and shook her head.

"I just love that people go caroling here."

"It's Reindeer Meadow," Kynlee reminded him. "I mean, I wouldn't be surprised if I saw little people with pointy ears and shoes running around making toys."

"No," Holly agreed with her. "You'd be drunk."

"Did you go caroling?" Kynlee shot her sister a grin and then turned her attention to Drake.

"Once. I think I was in third grade. Boy Scouts, maybe. We walked around a couple blocks by our school."

"We should go now," Holly mumbled. "You ready to play me again? For real this time?"

Kynlee shook her head. "Don't say things like that around him. He likes Christmas."

"So do I." Holly shrugged. "Most people do."

"Not everyone."

"She's just upset because when we were ten and eight, Santa brought us new bikes. Mine was purple. Hers was pink."

Drake turned to look at Kynlee, as if waiting for the punch line.

"Do I look like a pink kind of girl?" She tipped her head at him.

"Answer that correctly, or you'll be solo tomorrow night at the festival," Holly warned him.

"You absolutely do not strike me as a pink kind of girl."

"Thank you." Kynlee nodded.

"Anybody need another beer?" Brock asked.

"Oh, that's fair." Holly aimed a grin at him.

"Drake and I will have another beer, yes," Kynlee told Brock.

"She's bossy." Holly glanced at Drake.

"Noted."

"What do you do?" she asked him as Brock went upstairs to fetch the beers.

"IT stuff." He flinched suddenly and pulled his buzzing phone from his pocket. "And here we go."

Kynlee laughed softly. "Good luck."

He put the phone to his ear and wandered over by the tree. From the look on his face when he took the phone from his pocket, she assumed it was his mom.

"I can't believe he got over the bridge and then flipped his car."

Kynlee, chin ducked to her chest, lifted only her eyes to look at Holly.

"He could have just spent the night in Hannibal. I would assume the snow will stop one of these days."

Kynlee would agree, but if Drake had stopped in Hannibal, she wouldn't have met him.

Stunned by her thought, she froze for a moment, just as Holly dropped the ball into the game table.

So what if she wouldn't have met him? He was here for a day or two tops, and then he would be heading home. End of story.

Didn't matter that he was good-looking. And funny. And charming.

Charming?

Kynlee wasn't one to call anyone charming. In fact, she had probably never used the word before in her life. Holly whooped out loud again, snapping Kynlee out of her thoughts just in time to see the ball slide past her goalie again.

"Nope." She shook her head. "Wasn't ready."

"Tune it in, Kyn."

It wasn't like Overland Park was a thousand miles away. Kynlee had never been interested in long-distance relationships, but really, Overland Park wasn't that bad.

Relationships? Seriously? They'd joked about kissing and mistletoe. That hardly meant they were in a relationship.

"He's cute," Holly whispered.

"Stop it."

Brock returned with three longnecks and their parents in tow.

"How about a tournament?" Dad suggested.

"Sure, but Drake wants to go caroling."

"How about we do a round robin tournament?" Dad studied the game table. "And whoever's not playing can sing Christmas songs? Foosball and caroling."

"Oh my God." Kynlee closed her eyes and shook her head.

"What do you think, Drake?" Mom looked at Drake as he returned to the table.

"I don't know what I'm thinking about, but you're all fun, so I say yes to whatever's on the table."

Kynlee groaned.

"Okay." Dad nodded. "First up, Mom and Brock. Everybody else, "Here Comes Santa Claus." And hit it."

Dad, Holly, and Drake started singing instantly. Kynlee only rolled her eyes.

"And if you don't sing when you're supposed to, you do a solo after the game." Holly pointed at Kynlee.

CHAPTER TWELVE

"You didn't have to drive me," Drake told her as they climbed into the cab of her truck. Kynlee had used the remote start feature, so the interior was cozy warm. She buckled her seatbelt and then looked up at him.

"It would have been a long walk."

"Still." He shrugged.

"I don't mind," she told him. And then, as if she was afraid she had said too much, she cleared her throat and glanced over her shoulder. She put the truck in reverse and slowly backed out of the driveway. "Besides, I'm going home anyway."

Drake nodded and looked out his passenger window as she eased the truck onto the road and then put it in drive.

"Your family's fun."

She snorted softly. "They are."

"My mother wanted to ground me."

"For driving in a blizzard?" She peeked at him, but she was quick to turn her attention back to the road.

"Yep. Never mind that I'm okay."

"It could have been bad," she reminded him. "Don't do it again, okay?"

"Hmm." He tipped his head as he watched her drive.

"Hmm what?"

"Well, that's a long way from calling me an idiot."

She laughed softly. "I'm kind of opinionated," she mumbled. "And I don't have a filter."

"Noticed."

"And..." She took a deep breath and shrugged as she exhaled. "You're kind of fun. I wouldn't want you to end up injured in an accident."

"I'm kind of fun, huh?"

"I just hope you got the caroling thing out of the way." She sent him a frown that looked more like the woman he'd first met in Frosty's. "Because I won't be doing that on the streets of Reindeer Meadow."

"I think it would be fun," he answered.

"Living here....is..."

"What?"

"Well, I imagine it would be something like having your birthday close to Christmas. Your birthday should be special. And I have a friend whose birthday is Christmas Eve. Most people lump her birthday right in with Christmas. Like here's your presents. They cover both. Didn't have any birthday paper so I just used Christmas paper."

"Yeah, I get that," he answered with a nod. "My brother's birthday is two days after Christmas."

She nodded as if she was putting the matter to rest.

"But how is that like living in Reindeer Meadow?" He shook his head. "That comparison doesn't work."

Kynlee glanced at him.

"It's just...when you live in a place like this, you get lumped in with all the Christmas lovers and people just assume you love Christmas. And maybe you don't."

"Do you like other holidays?"

She laughed. "I like Thanksgiving."

"Yeah?"

"Yes. It's my favorite holiday."

"And do you celebrate birthdays?"

"I do, but I don't like gifts." She shrugged. "I don't like the spotlight."

"Amusement parks?"

"What?"

"Do you like amusement parks?"

"No." She narrowed her eyes at him and shook her head. "That transition was as smooth as my birthday comparison."

"Why don't you like amusement parks?"

"Because." She sighed. "I mean, look at everything that could go wrong."

"You said you weren't afraid of anything."

"I'm not," she argued. "I'm sensible. What if the engineer designing a roller coaster has an off day? And there's a flaw in the design. And someone is seriously injured or killed?"

"And the pink bike? Is that a true story?"

"See? You can't argue with me about roller coasters."

"I don't care for them," he admitted. "They hurt my back. And spinny rides make me sick."

She grinned and shook her head. "I did get a pink bike when I was eight. And while I loved riding my bike, I don't love pink."

"And?"

"Well, I was eight, and I was a brat. And I was mouthy about the pink bike."

"And that's why you don't like Christmas?"

Kynlee chewed on her lip as she slowed to a stop in front of Cecil's place. She put the truck in park and turned to look at him.

"After Christmas break, when we went back to school, I told my friends about the pink bike. And there was this girl in my class. Her dad wasn't in the picture. Her mom..." She cleared her throat. "Things were bad. Hard for them. That girl was a spitfire. She was always mean. She had a colorful vocabulary and a mean right hook."

"She was eight?"

"Yeah." Kynlee nodded. "She heard me talking to my friends about the bike. And she told me I was the most selfish, ugliest person she knew."

Drake flinched. "Kids say things, Kynlee. You know that."

"I do." She nodded. "But I also know that she was right. I had everything under the sun. And she had nothing. But I had the nerve to complain about the color of my bike."

He started to argue, to remind her that eight-year-olds could be immature, due to the fact that they were indeed eight years old. Childish. Selfish. But Kynlee shook her head.

"That stuck with me. I don't want to be that person."

"Okay." He nodded. "I get that."

She looked away, studied something through the windshield for a moment before looking back at him.

"What time are we doing this date tomorrow?"

"I'm free all day," he reminded her.

"No fancy working to do on your laptop?"

"No." He shook his head. "Nothing that can't wait."

"I'd be super impressed," she quirked an eyebrow at him, "but I know you don't have a good internet connection here."

With a laugh, Drake unbuckled his seatbelt.

"If you're not plowing driveways tomorrow, what will you do?"

"You want me to say something like making snow angels, don't you?"

"I think you would make snow devils," he answered with a grin. "Cute ones. Little bit ornery looking."

They stared at each other in silence for a moment. He was going to kiss her. Mistletoe or not.

"Give me your number," he said quietly.

She rattled it off before he even had his phone out of his pocket and laughed when he flicked his gaze up to meet her eyes.

"Joke's on you," he said as he tapped his screen and entered her number into his contacts. "Good memory."

"Come over for breakfast," she told him.

Surprised at her invitation, Drake could only nod.

"Where?"

Again, she rattled off her address. Drake simply nodded. He wouldn't forget.

Her eyes grew wide as he leaned closer to brush his lips over hers.

"Did you tell your mom there's a delay with getting your car taken care of?"

"I did."

"Did you tell her I offered to drive you in to Hannibal so you could rent something and get home for Christmas?"

Her whispered words brushed over his lips as he leaned close again.

"No. I told her I wasn't sure I would make it home this year."

CHAPTER THIRTEEN

Drake Palmer saw her.

Yeah, he'd gotten the pink question right when they were playing foosball with her family.

But that little comment in her truck last night, the thing about her making snow devils? That touched her. He wasn't saying she was evil. Simply that if she were to go outside and take part in a silly activity that other people did around the holidays, she would leave a different imprint in the snow.

Because she was a little bit snarky, a little rough around the edges.

And he had kissed her.

Twice.

Which she was pretty sure meant that he didn't mind her rough edges.

He knocked on her door after nine. Kynlee had already made a pot of coffee, and she had muffins in the oven. She told herself as she hurried through her living room to get the door that she wasn't trying to impress him. It didn't matter that he knew she could cook. She was simply being nice to someone stranded in Reindeer Meadow.

"Hey." She offered him a smile when she pulled the door open. "C'min."

"Thanks." He stomped his feet outside the door before coming inside.

"How was the walk?" she asked him. Drake unbuttoned his coat and slipped it off his shoulders.

"Nice, actually," he answered. "It stopped snowing."

"I saw that." She took his coat as he slipped his shoes off.

"Calvin Grady called this morning."

Kynlee hoped she hid her flinch from Drake. If Calvin called, that might mean he had pulled Drake's car from the side of the road. Drake could be headed home by lunch time. She hated to see him leave.

On the other hand, if he was stranded here, she couldn't be sure he would *want* to be here.

"What's the word on your car?"

"They towed it in. But some of the fluids are compromised. And there's extensive damage to the body. His opinion is that insurance will want to total it."

Kynlee laid his coat over the back of her couch and led him into the kitchen.

"Wow." She cleared her throat and took a deep breath. A little unsettled—more at the thought of how badly he could have been injured than worried about his vehicle and what it meant for him for the holidays—she waved her hand at the coffee maker and looked at him.

When he nodded, she filled the mug she had already set out for him.

"I'm just glad you're okay, Drake," she said quietly as she handed the mug to him. "Do you need cream or sugar?"

"No, thanks."

Their fingers didn't touch accidentally; rather, Drake made a point of brushing his fingers over hers.

"Um." She reminded herself he was here for breakfast. "Okay. I have cranberry orange muffins in the oven. Bacon and eggs?"

"Wow." He flashed her a grin. "You cook."

"Yes, I can cook." She felt the blush rush her cheeks. "I grew up in Liz Austin's house."

"It sounds good."

She nodded, and they stood for a moment sharing a goofy, syrupy grin.

"Gotta do this first." He put his mug on the counter and stepped closer to her. Kynlee tipped her head back as he rested his hands on her hips. "Is this okay?"

"Yes."

This kiss was a little different from those last night in her truck. He lingered there at her lips a little longer. When he did press his to her mouth, she kissed him back. The taste of his mint toothpaste made her a little giddy.

"Why are you laughing?" he whispered when she chuckled against his lips.

"Just thinking that you taste fresh and minty, and that it's been a long time since I've been kissed."

"See?" He stepped back and picked up his mug again. "If you had mistletoe around, that might change."

"Sit." She nodded at the bar as she went to the fridge for the bacon and eggs. "I don't want mistletoe around."

"Right." He sighed. "No Christmas stuff here."

She looked around her kitchen, a stab of disappointment in her belly. She didn't decorate for Christmas. She never had. Coming home to her simple, everyday house, out of the holiday craziness had always been her sanctuary. Now it made her a little bit sad.

It wasn't the Christmas thing that had made her say she didn't want mistletoe around, though. She didn't want just anyone kissing her. She liked the way Drake Palmer kissed her.

"What're you gonna do about your car?"

"I dunno." He shrugged. "I guess I need to call my insurance company and have someone come and take a look at it first."

"Except that it's Friday, two days before Christmas."

"Right." He nodded.

"My offer stands."

"Driving me to Hannibal so I can rent a car and get home for Christmas?"

"Yep."

She held her breath for a moment, not sure what she wanted him to say. *Yes, he wanted to go home, or no, he would just ride the holidays out here, so he could deal with the car after Christmas?*

If being with his family was that important to him, shouldn't Kynlee want him to get home and see them?

"Thanks," he said with a nod. Uncertain what his thanks meant, Kynlee simply nodded as she cracked an egg over a bowl. "Scrambled okay?"

"Yes."

"Good."

"What if I told you I wanted you to do something for me?"

"Just told you I'd drive you to Hannibal," she reminded him.

"As my Christmas gift."

Kynlee shot him a look since he seemed to be ignoring her.

"What?"

"Let's go pick out a little Christmas tree."

"For what? Your room at Cecil's?"

"For your house."

"Why would I want a tree here?"

"I just think you would like it once it was here."

Kynlee took a deep breath and worked quietly for a few minutes.

"Are you planning to stick around for Christmas?"

"Are you going to agree to get a tree and then take it down the second I leave?"

She laughed softly. "I wouldn't do that."

"I think I'd like to spend Christmas here," he answered. "With you."

"But?"

"But you don't celebrate Christmas," he reminded her.

"But you get why I don't."

"I do." He nodded. "But I..."

"What?"

"What if you celebrated Christmas for other people?"

"I do." She tipped her head and waggled her eyebrows. "My family."

"I know." He nodded. "But I meant, what if you, like, picked a family to buy for. To give them a Christmas."

Kynlee stilled her hands over the skillet and studied him for a second.

"Like, instead of getting gifts, you spend your Christmas being Santa to someone else? Who wouldn't have a Christmas?"

She swallowed hard.

"I mean, from what I gather, you do things for people all the time. It's okay to give someone else a Christmas and feel good about it."

"I wouldn't want anyone to know it was me."

"No one would have to know." He shrugged. "What do you think?"

"I'm intrigued."

"It's just that as my brothers and I have gotten older, we don't need all the expensive gifts. Ya know? Game consoles. Speaker systems. Whatever. My parents always said that finding the perfect gift for someone was the magical part of Christmas. I get it now that I'm older."

The oven beeped. Kynlee turned away from him and grabbed the oven mitt from the counter.

"My dad loves bourbon and barrels and the bourbon trail. Two years ago, Mom got him a watch made from bourbon barrels. She was so excited about giving it to him. He could have given her a pair of socks, and she still would have been thrilled, because he loved his gift."

Kynlee considered what Drake said as she selected plates and forks and put them on the counter by him.

"Help yourself," she said quietly.

Drake kissed her cheek as he reached for a plate.

"I am."

CHAPTER FOURTEEN

HE COULDN'T BELIEVE HE TALKED HER INTO GOING TO THE TREE farm, that she'd given in so easily. Then again, Drake got the feeling that Kynlee loved to do things for others, so his argument had apparently hit the mark. He would feel guilty for it, but how could he when he truly believed she would enjoy Christmas if she were the one giving to others? Even if it was only her time, if she thought of it that way, that she was doing something for someone else, she would enjoy it and come to appreciate the season.

The Fayrweather Tree Farm didn't disappoint. With the rest of Reindeer Valley being the perfect small Christmas town, Drake had pictured a wooden sign bearing the name of the property. He had been delighted to see not only a wooden sign, but that sign wrapped with white Christmas lights. A small building just inside the picket fence that surrounded the farm, also decorated for Christmas with lights and fake snow in the windows, looked warm and inviting.

"You should see it at night," Kynlee said as they walked past the sign through the entrance. "All lit up."

"Yeah?" He gave her the side eye.

She laughed softly. "It's pretty," she admitted.

"What's in there?" He nodded toward the building.

"Homemade cookies. Hot chocolate. Tree ornaments. Other decorations."

"So, it's the hub of the place."

"Yeah, I guess it is."

"Is that where we go for a saw? Do we cut our own tree down?"

Kynlee's smile was small, skittish, but he saw it before she looked away.

"We can. Or we can have one of their workers do it."

"I think we should try it."

"What if the tree falls on us and one of is injured?"

"Are you always into the worst-case scenario?"

She ducked her head. "I suppose I am."

"Live a little, Kynlee." He bumped her arm with his elbow.

Drake pulled the door open and ushered her inside in front of him. A fireplace in the far corner of the building boasted pretty flames and made the building cozy warm. There were several trees decorated; Drake assumed the ornaments on the trees were for sale. A table in front of the counter held small games and puzzles for sale. Two women and a young kid seemed to be moving everywhere at once, busy doing something.

"Kynlee?" One of the women did a double take as they approached the counter. While Drake understood her surprise, he wished she wouldn't make a big deal of Kynlee being there.

But Kynlee only smiled and shrugged. "I know, right?"

"What're you up to?"

"Um." Kynlee glanced at Drake with a smile. "My friend here wants a Christmas tree."

"Yeah? Is he gonna put it up in his room at Cecil's?"

Drake hoped his surprise didn't show on his face. It was easy to forget this was a small town and everyone here knew everyone else's business.

"It's actually going to my house," Kynlee said simply.

"I hope lightning doesn't strike your house once it's all done."

Drake winced, but Kynlee laughed.

"Okay." The woman behind the counter nodded, as if she was ready to get down to business. "Want Jaden to cut it down for you? Or are you guys gonna do it?"

"We're gonna do it," Drake answered for Kynlee.

"Perfect." The woman turned away from them and selected a crosscut saw from a hook on the wall. She laid it on the counter and grabbed a clipboard with a paper on it. Drake assumed it was a waiver saying the tree farm wasn't responsible if he or Kynlee was injured while using their saw.

"How're Harold and Edna?" Kynlee asked as he scribbled his name on the form.

"They're good." The woman nodded and took the clipboard from him. "Ready for Christmas."

"How's Doug's little boy?"

Drake noticed the sadness slide into Kynlee's expression, weighing her cheeks down a bit and making her eyes look almost glassy.

"Good days and bad," the woman answered.

"Tell them all hello."

"Will do."

The woman turned her attention back to Drake. "Grab a pair of gloves unless you want blisters."

"I think I'll pass on the blisters, thanks." He smiled as he snatched a pair of work gloves off a shelf to the side of the counter.

"Good hunting," the woman called as he and Kynlee headed back outside.

"Here we go." He smiled at Kynlee when she looked up at him. Today, she wore her Carhartt again. Skinny jeans. Big snow boots—Drake glanced at his shoes with a sigh. They would be ruined when this trip was over. And his feet were already cold. But he didn't care. He and Kynlee were about to cut down a tree. Talk about a Christmas adventure.

"The property is huge."

"How's it work? Divided by age of trees? Types?"

She snorted. "Like I would know? I haven't been out here in over twenty years."

"Do you have ornaments?" he asked her as they walked down a row of trees. Drake breathed deeply, inhaling the scent of the evergreens.

"Um. No." She shook her head. "But my parents have some we can steal."

"Oh. Adding burglary to our Christmas adventure." He laughed and shrugged. "I like it."

"So. What's the story with Doug's little boy?"

"Mmm." She flinched. "I went to school with Doug. He's a Fayrweather. Has three kids. His youngest boy is four. He has leukemia."

"I'm sorry to hear that."

Kynlee nodded. "They're good people."

"Like that tree?" He pointed at a tree that had to be at least twelve foot tall, simply to make her smile.

"Sure. Think it'll fit in my little living room?"

"I'm sure it would," he answered, her laugh warming him from inside. "The problem would be cutting it down."

"How does it work?"

"Don't know. Never done this before."

"What?" She grabbed his arm as they walked, laughing but obviously a little worried.

"Haven't. But my brother and his wife do it every year. If he can do it, I can."

"Oh boy." She rolled her eyes. "This should be interesting."

"Just don't record me and post it on social media."

"If I had social media accounts, you can bet I'd be posting that all over them."

"No social media, huh?"

"Nope." She shrugged. "Life's too short to stare at a screen all the time."

Drake linked his fingers with hers. "Another thing I like about you."

"If it's another, then there's at least two things you like about me." She tipped her head to look up at him.

"There's a lot of things I like about you," he agreed. "What do you think of that little tree right behind you?"

She spun around and then stared silently for a moment. Drake guessed the tree to be about four feet tall. Skinny enough for her house, but big enough to make a pretty tree once it was decorated.

"I like it," she said quietly.

"I'm sorry. What did you say?" He stepped up beside her and looked at her with a grin.

"I like it," she said again. "I like the tree. I like your idea of giving someone else Christmas. And..."

"And what?" He let his eyes roam over her face. Her cheeks were pink with the cold, and her eyes shined in the bright sunlight. Drake held his breath for a moment, almost glad that he'd wrecked his car. That the tow-truck had been down yesterday from its own collision. And that Mother

Nature had dumped a ton of snow right here in Reindeer Meadow, Illinois.

The perfect storm.

"I like you."

Before he could move, Kynlee turned and grabbed his upper arms. She dropped a peck on his lips and then stepped back to eye the tree.

"Okay, Mr. Lumberjack. Let's see you cut down this tree."

CHAPTER FIFTEEN

It was surprisingly easy. Drake even insisted that Kynlee take a few strokes with the saw. They laughed together as he knelt in the snow, holding the tree with one hand, and her tugging the glove off his other hand. Drake did the bulk of the work, slow and particular, not to mention that they were squished in between more trees in all directions.

When they were finished, Jaden Fayrweather appeared as if by magic to help them. Drake dropped the saw and took the tree from where Kynlee was holding onto it. He gave it a shake. Kynlee saw a few needles fall, but there weren't many. Jaden helped Drake get the tree over to the sled he had brought down with him and promised he would get it up to the building and tag it for them.

"What'd you think?" Drake looked up at her as he reached down to get the saw.

"I think you're ruining your shoes," she answered simply.

He glanced at the wet, brown leather, snow caked on the toes, and shrugged.

"Worth it."

Kynlee took a deep breath, loving the scent of fresh pine.

"What kind of tree was it?" she asked him.

"Balsam fir."

"You know that from looking?"

"Nope." He grinned. "Saw the little sign at the front of the row."

"I haven't decorated a tree since I left for college."

"It's like riding a bike," he promised her. "It'll come back to you."

"Nice." She laughed softly.

"Ready to go break into your parents' house and steal ornaments?"

"You make it sound so exciting."

Together, they walked back up the lane toward the building. More people lingered around the door now, but Kynlee didn't see many out looking at trees. Because, as she well knew, most people in Reindeer Meadow got their fresh trees in the beginning of December.

Inside the little mercantile building, they looked at the ornaments hanging on the display trees. There were glass ornaments, plastic ornaments that wouldn't break, bells, sleds, mangers—anything and everything Kynlee could imagine hung from one of the trees. She had to laugh when she saw a cut out of red lawnmower. Her mom had a few of those on the tree at her house, because of the landscaping business.

"These are neat." Drake pointed at a section of ornaments to be personalized.

"They are." She glanced at them with a nod. Her parents had those sorts of ornaments, too, and they had given Holly and Brock a couple through the years.

"Want to get one?"

"And put what on it?" She tipped her head to look at him, hoping her question didn't sound as confrontational as it felt.

"You could just put the year on it," he suggested.

She could. But she wasn't wild about the idea.

"Or you could put my name on it and always remember the year you met the idiot who drove his car off the road for Christmas."

Kynlee snorted and shrugged. "I could."

She watched him select a Christmas tree with two red gifts under it. Before he could say more, she took the tree from him and carried it to the counter.

"That all for you?" Donna Wilson, the woman she had talked to before going outside, asked her. "This and the four-foot Balsam?"

"Yeah. Can I get that personalized?"

"Of course." Donna nodded and picked up a black felt tip marker.

"The year here." She pointed to the bottom of the tree trunk. "Drake here. Kynlee here."

"You're gonna start rumors," Donna warned her.

"Any rumors that start will come from you." Kynlee pointed at her, but she smiled. "And it seemed nicer than saying the year the idiot drove his car off the road."

Drake pulled his wallet out and selected a credit card.

"You don't have to buy it."

"I wanted you to have a tree," he reminded her. "And if it's a one-time thing for you, I'll take the ornament when I leave."

"So you can remember the year you met the grinchette?"

"Exactly." He nodded and took the card back from Donna. He scribbled his name on the receipt and handed it back to Donna.

"Jaden's already got it in your truck, Kynlee."

"Thank you."

"Merry Christmas."

Kynlee nodded, feeling Drake's eyes on her. "Merry Christmas to you, too."

"Is that new?" he asked as they walked back out to the truck.

"What?"

"Someone wishing you a Merry Christmas?"

"Mm. No."

"Does it make you twitch when they do?"

She laughed and looked at him over the bed of the truck. "No."

"Okay. Well, let's go crash your parents' house."

Kynlee drove straight to her parents' house and led him to the basement again to the storage area. Her dad kept this area so organized it took her less than five minutes to find a box of Christmas things they didn't use anymore. Drake carried the box to the truck as Kynlee texted her mom to tell her they had borrowed the decorations.

She knew she would hear about it—not that her parents would care. But they would certainly tease her about putting up a tree just because this guy had wanted her to. At her house, he pulled the tree so that the base of it hung over the tailgate and then used a saw she had in her little garage to trim it again and put it in the tree stand she'd taken from her parents' house.

Once the tree was relatively straight, Kynlee opened her front door and watched as Drake carried it inside. They had decided before going to the farm that she should put the tree in front of her window, so Drake put it there now and then stepped back to eyeball it with her.

"Look okay?"

She tipped her head this way and that to study it and finally nodded.

"I think so."

Drake did the same before agreeing with her.

"Okay. I'll bring the ornaments in. You water the tree."

"Aye, aye captain."

He laughed and rolled his eyes as he headed back out the front door and she went to get water for the tree. While they decorated the tree, Drake played Christmas music on his phone. He asked if she cared, and while she hadn't been excited about it, she didn't mind. But once they were hanging ornaments and sharing memories—Drake had two stories to every one she told since she still felt that reluctance to let go and have fun for the holidays—she found herself warming to the classic songs her parents had always listened to.

It didn't take long to finish the tree, and once Drake put the star topper on it, they both stood back to admire their work. No tinsel or garland, but a red velvet ribbon wrapped around the tree added a pretty pop of color. The old ornaments brought back some memories for Kynlee from when she and Holly were little girls.

Drake was right, she supposed. She loved her family, and they did always have fun during the holidays. Just because she didn't want to receive gifts didn't mean she couldn't still celebrate Christmas.

And the idea of wrapping up a nice, needed Christmas for a less fortunate family had grown on her all day while they worked. She was too late to do it this year; after all, tomorrow was Christmas Eve. But she would do it next year. The next several months would give her plenty of time to choose a family to help.

"You know what I was hoping for?" Drake asked her.

Standing side by side in front of the tree, Kynlee turned to look up at him. "What?"

"To find that contraband mistletoe in the box."

She laughed and leaned into him when he slid his arms around her waist.

"Darn."

"If I had some, would you kiss me?"

"I would."

"And am I better kisser than sixteen-year-old Brad Young?"

"How do you even remember his name?"

"Guys remember important things."

"How's his name important?" She rested her hands on his shoulders.

"Well, you were making out with him under mistletoe. And you said you didn't like it. I need to make sure I've got game. That I'm a better kisser than that guy."

"Hmm." She nodded. "I see what you mean."

"And?"

"I don't know." She tipped her head and narrowed her eyes at him. "I'm thinking I need more kisses before I can make that call."

CHAPTER SIXTEEN

EVEN THOUGH DRAKE WON THE FOOSBALL GAME, THEY WENT FOR dinner before going to the Christmas festival. There wasn't a lot of variety in Reindeer Meadow, so they had a pepperoni pizza and a couple of beers before heading out to the square. As far as Drake was concerned, it was the best date he'd had in ages.

Maybe ever.

But then the last two days with Kynlee were unlike most days in his life, definitely his adult life. He worked. He traveled for work. Now and then he went out for dinner or attended a party with a friend of a friend. But he had never felt so at ease and at the same time so excited about spending time with a woman the way he did with Kynlee.

Riding around Reindeer Meadow with her yesterday had been a blast. She was a little bit quirky and slightly grumpy, but he loved it. She made him laugh. And as grouchy as she might claim to be, she had laughed at and with him, and *that* was a big deal to Drake.

Last night with her family had been fun. Reminiscent of the fun things his family did together. She would fit in with his brothers, with his parents and sister-in-law. They would like her. Drake found himself wishing he could take her home with him and introduce her. And that thought made him laugh. Kynlee would probably throat punch him if he so much as hinted at that. It was one thing for him to be stuck here in Reindeer Meadow, to have met her family as he did. Quite another thing for him to take her home to meet his family after being around her for two days.

"So, what do we do here?" Drake asked her as they walked through the square. "Are they bobbing for apples?" He stopped walking and watched two kids hanging their heads over a metal bucket.

"Yes."

"Seriously?" he yelped. "First of all, I have never seen anyone do that. Ever. And second, it's way too cold for that!"

"Ever heard of the polar bear plunge?" Kynlee looked up at him.

She had changed into a deep green sweater and a long, camel-colored wool coat. Though she still wore snow boots, these were different. Smaller. Daintier. Her lips were shiny with some kind of gloss, and her eyes shined like diamonds.

"You're beautiful." He reached for her hand. "Do you know that?"

"No." She shook her head.

"You are." With a shrug, he kissed the top of her head. "Oops. People are going to be whispering now."

"Nah." She shook her head. "They won't whisper. And they're already talking. After all, a stranger comes to town, and now Kynlee Austin has a Christmas tree in her window."

"Christmas miracle, huh?"

She laughed. "Something like that."

He started walking again, but he stopped when she didn't move.

"What?"

"Thought you might wanna get in line to bob for apples."

"I think I'll pass."

"Okay." She shrugged. "Fudge?"

"I could do a little piece of fudge."

They wandered from booth to booth, talking to people Kynlee had apparently known most of her life. They sampled ciders and mulled wines, fudge, and candied pecans. Drake marveled at the fact that the woman who claimed to not like Christmas was so comfortable—no, it was more than that. Kynlee was having fun, even if she didn't want to admit it. Her smile was far too warm to be anything but genuine. She called everyone by name and asked after grandparents and grandchildren and dogs. Drake heard several people thank her for taking care of their driveways and walking their dogs and delivering baked goodies her mom had made at Frosty's.

She claimed she didn't like Christmas, and she claimed she wasn't afraid of anything. But Drake saw both of those statements. Maybe she was afraid of having fun, afraid of that greedy little kid who opened her mouth and said the wrong thing, as kids often do, when she was in school. Maybe the mean girl who had called her out had handed her a sense of duty to the community. And Drake could see she enjoyed being part of the community. It was obvious helping people did make her happy.

And yet, she seemed to believe she had to dislike Christmas, because otherwise it made her selfish.

"Do you wanna go ice skating?" she asked him after a while.

"No." He shook his head. "I would love to see the rink, but I'll stay on solid ground, thanks."

She looked up at him with a smile. "Flipping your car was enough excitement for you?"

"Yes, enough for the rest of my life," he answered.

Kynlee squeezed his fingers. "I'm glad you're okay."

Eyes locked, they stood for a moment. Drake would have been happy to stand there looking at her forever, but someone came up behind him and drew Kynlee's attention away.

"So, what's this I hear about a Christmas tree in your living room window?"

Drake turned to see Holly and Brock, both wearing big smiles.

"I did it for him." Kynlee nodded at Drake.

"Yeah?" Holly glanced at him. "Are you staying for Christmas?"

He wanted to stay for Christmas. As much as he would miss his family, he wanted to stay here and celebrate with Kynlee. And no, he didn't want to play Scrabble or foosball and share a Christmas toast and then walk away considering her a friend.

Drake wanted more. Kynlee had been flirty, and she had been in the moment with him for the kisses. But he had no idea what she was thinking. He glanced at her before answering, wishing she would say that she wanted him to stay.

"I don't know."

"I told him the offer's open to rent a car and get home."

"And yet, he hasn't taken you up on it." Holly arched her eyebrows and shrugged. "Imagine that."

Drake met Holly's eyes and smiled. He knew where she stood on the issue. Why couldn't Kynlee be easier to read? Then again, that mystery was part of what drew him to her.

Holly, wearing a red wool coat and matching red boots, threw her arm around Kynlee's shoulders. Together, they looked very Christmassy, like elves. Drake caught himself before he snorted out loud. If Kynlee could read his mind, she would probably drag him to her truck and drive him to Hannibal immediately.

"Seen Mom and Dad?" Kynlee asked her sister.

"They were getting mulled wine."

"I was going to show Drake the ice-skating rink."

"Break a leg." Holly nodded and leaned into Brock. "Don't really, though. Be hard to coach your girls with a cast on your leg."

"We're not skating." Kynlee shook her head. "Just walking around."

"Sounds romantic." Holly winked at him. She and Brock started walking. "See you in a bit."

"Romantic," Drake repeated as he and Kynlee headed away from the square.

"Sorry."

"You don't like romance, either?"

"I don't know," she answered thoughtfully. "I can't say that anyone I've dated has been really romantic."

"Not even Brad the sixteen-year-old mistletoe abuser?"

"Stop it." She laughed and shook her head.

"Did you decide? Who's the better—"

"You are. You know that."

CHAPTER SEVENTEEN

He hadn't taken her up on the offer of a ride into Hannibal. Did that mean something? Did she want it to mean something?

She did. Kynlee was beyond lying to herself about it. While she had dated plenty, she hadn't ever been so much in love she wanted to settle down. It was early, obviously, to say she was in love with Drake. But she was in something. And she wanted to explore whatever it was she was feeling that he might be feeling.

What if she just asked him to stay?

But he had family he wanted to be with, and his life was in Overland Park.

"What're you thinking about?" His deep voice nudged her out of her thoughts. Eyes on the ice-skaters, she shrugged and shook her head.

"Nothing."

So, she wasn't brave. Courageous. She could handle the snow all day long, and she wasn't physically afraid of any man she'd ever met. She and Holly had taken Tae Kwon Do lessons when they were young girls, and they knew how to defend themselves. Kynlee was strong, tough.

But she was afraid to ask Drake Palmer to stay for Christmas.

Did she really think he would say no?

Or was she suspicious of why he would say yes?

"Kynlee."

She turned her head to look at him when he said her name.

"What're you thinking?"

"You."

"Me?"

"Yeah."

"What about me?"

"That I feel bad you're not gonna be home for Christmas."

She watched emotions flicker over his face, unable to label any, uncertain what he was thinking.

"It's not your fault," he reminded her.

"Yeah, but you're here trying to make me feel the magic of Christmas, and I can't do anything for you."

"You could." He nodded.

Kynlee licked her lips as she met his eyes. "What?"

Drake sighed and looked around. "Let's walk."

She nodded and fell into step beside him.

"They'll be singing soon," she announced.

"Who?"

"There's always a couple of groups who sing. Some school kids."

"How about the ladies' group who carols and shoots pool?"

She laughed and shrugged. "Maybe."

"Do they wear leather vests?"

"Like a motorcycle club?"

"Yes!"

"No." She shook her head. "That's weird."

"When they sing..."

She looked at him expectantly.

"At the festival."

She nodded to show she was following him.

"Does everyone sing along?"

"You still want to go caroling, don't you?"

"Not if we get to sing along tonight."

"Usually, we end the night with a sing-along to 'We Wish You a Merry Christmas.' Does that work?"

"It'll do, I guess. I want to hear Rudolph."

She wanted to touch his face. Slide her hand over his cheek. Touch the dimple beside his lips. But she made herself behave.

"What can I give you? For Christmas?"

Kynlee watched his eyes grow wide again as they neared the square again. Even though he had already seen it all, he was like a little kid, drinking it all again, like it was the first time. She loved the look of wonder on his face and wished she could feel that way about the holidays.

The thing of it was, she thought she might. If he were always a part of them.

"You really don't know?"

His voice was a little gruff. From across the street, a group of young voices started singing "Frosty the Snowman." But Drake was firmly in the moment with her and didn't even seem to hear the song.

"I don't." She shook her head.

"Ask me to stay."

"What?"

"Ask me to stay with you. For Christmas."

Her mouth was suddenly dry, and she tried several times to speak. She couldn't find her voice.

"Or would you rather drive me to Hannibal and stick me in a rental car bound for Overland Park?"

She laughed softly and shook her head.

"I want you to stay."

"Because I made you put up a Christmas tree?"

"Because you make me happy. Even here. In Reindeer Meadow."

"That's saying something pretty big." He tipped his head. "You sure?"

"I'm sure."

"And if I kiss you right now and everyone sees us? You're okay with that?"

"Yes." She grinned.

"Even if I kiss you with lots of tongue?"

She laughed and swatted at him, leaving her hand to rest on his chest. "If you say his name—"

"I am more than happy to forget he ever existed if you are."

"I am."

"Let's go sing along," he suggested.

"Wait." She grabbed a fistful of his coat.

"What?"

"Will you? Stay? For Christmas?"

"Yes."

She swallowed hard and licked her lips, nervous about her next question.

"Will you move your things from Cecil's? And stay with me?"

"I will."

"Good."

She opened her mouth again, ready to ask him to kiss her. But Drake swooped in close.

"Stop talking, woman!"

"Kiss me."

"I'm trying."

He kissed her. With a lot of heat and emotion. And tongue.

"Let's go sing." She pulled back to look at him and quirked an eyebrow.

"You? Wanna sing?"

She laughed softly and nodded. "I do. With you."

Hand in hand, they crossed the street and wound through the crowd of people gathered by the little homemade wooden stage they used every year in the square for the festival. Kynlee worked her way through the crowd, Drake on her heels, until she found her sister and brother-in-law standing with their parents.

The caroling ladies sang next. Drake slipped his arm around her shoulders when they started the song "It's Beginning to Look a Lot Like Christmas." Kynlee looked up at him as she started singing.

CHAPTER EIGHTEEN

"My favorite ever?" Drake asked. Lying together on the couch, facing the tree they had decorated together, he looped his arm around her waist.

"Yeah. Favorite present ever?"

"Hmm." He dropped his head back to rest on the couch and closed his eyes. "Toss up. Either the football signed by a college player I thought was awesome when I was fifteen."

"Really?"

"I was fifteen," he reminded her with a shrug. "Kinda like—"

With a laugh, Kynlee lifted her hand and covered his mouth with her fingers. "Shh."

"It was cool."

"Okay, so either that or what?"

"Going to the Christmas tree farm with you and cutting down a tree."

Kynlee scooched around on the couch so she was lying flat on her back. Drake draped his leg over hers and dropped a kiss on her cheek.

"It was kind of fun," she admitted.

"Totally worth ruining my shoes."

"I'll get you new ones," she promised with a smile.

"It's not a long drive."

"What's not?"

"Here to Overland Park."

"What about Overland Park to here?"

He grinned. "Probably about the same. Doncha think?"

"You're gonna drive here to take me out to dinner?"

"I will." He nodded. "Will you drive to see me?"

"Of course," she answered. "Considering that right now you don't have a vehicle."

"Still think I'm an idiot?"

"No." She smoothed her fingers over his lips and shook her head. "I'm just glad you weren't seriously injured."

"What if one day I moved here?"

"To Reindeer Meadow?" She shook her head. "No. No way."

"No?"

"What if one day I moved to Overland Park?" she asked with a smile. "And we could come here and visit during the holidays?"

"You'd leave Reindeer Meadow for me?"

Kynlee snorted and looked back at the tree.

"I've never spent Christmas Eve like this," she told him.

"How do you usually spend it?"

"At my parents' house. Eating. Watching movies. Cooking for Christmas day."

"Regrets?" He touched her cheek and then traced a line over her lips.

"No."

"Do you go to church?"

"Yeah. We always walk over to Immaculate Conception for midnight mass."

"Nice." He nodded. "We used to do that. But then my older brother got married. Now they have Addison. So they stopped going on Christmas Eve. They go Christmas morning. So my parents started going to an earlier mass on Christmas Eve."

"That reminds me." She smiled. "I'm gonna be an aunt."

"You are."

"That might mean I have to believe in Santa Claus again."

"Yes!" Drake leaned over and stole a kiss. "You will have to believe in Santa again."

"Maybe I already do," she whispered.

"What if I said I love you?"

"Too soon. If you say it now, I'd assume it was the legend of the Fayrweather farm."

"What if it was? You're pure in heart. You deserve someone to love you."

"But to me, that's like giving you a love potion."

"Nope, that's different. Because it could be anyone. Giving the potion. Drinking it. Falling for anyone. Too random. What if the Fayrweather legend worked because you're pure in heart, and I'm the one for you?"

She grinned.

"I like your confidence."

"I like your everything," he said simply.

"Tell me on a different day."

"Well, I guess Valentine's Day is out. And St. Patrick's Day is out."

"Why St. Patrick's Day?"

"Because you would accuse me of getting drunk with a leprechaun or something and mistaking my lust for you as love."

"Are leprechauns lusty creatures?"

"What about April?"

"Well, not April Fool's Day." She rolled her eyes. Drake laughed out loud.

"May twenty-sixth," he decided.

"Why? What's special about May twenty-sixth?"

"It's the day I'm going to profess my love for you. Is that acceptable?"

Kynlee pushed herself up and rested on her elbow.

"I think that's a very acceptable date," she whispered. Pressing a kiss to his lips, she drew back and met his eyes. "But it's also way too far away."

"I love that you're impossible."

"And I love that you don't give up."

EPILOGUE

ONE YEAR LATER

"Ready?"

Kynlee glanced at Drake across the cab of his truck. Head tipped back to rest on the seat, he drummed his fingers on the steering wheel to the beat of an instrumental Christmas song by August Burns Red.

"Are you?" she asked him.

He offered her a lazy grin and then looked out the driver's window at the snow. Not like it was last year, when they had first met. But there was a fresh blanket of white over the ground.

"Let's do it." He nodded and turned the truck ignition off.

Kynlee zipped her coat up and pulled her beanie down low over her head. The truck was cozy warm; they had been parked down the road now for a while, watching and waiting. Two of the three houses on this street were empty; nature had come to claim both. Weeds nearly as tall as a toddler encroached on one, tall and strong enough to pop up through the snow. The other had cracked windows, a tree limb sticking through one, and Kynlee guessed maybe several animal families living in it.

The Walters family lived in the third house—a young husband and wife and two little kids. The husband had been severely injured on the job, and his wife was working at Berry's now. But Kynlee knew they were scrambling to get by. She'd talked to Amy at Berry's more than once. The girl was probably a good five years younger than her, but life had aged her. She looked permanently exhausted and sad.

The kids, five and three, were adorable. Kynlee had seen them around town often enough. The five-year-old was a curly-haired hellion who liked toy cars. Rumor had it the three-year-old didn't talk. It had been a no-brainer for Kynlee that she wanted to help the Walters family for Christmas. She and Drake had been doing the long-distance relationship for a year now; both talked often about changing that, changing someone's location. But with the thrill of new love and road tripping back and forth to see each other, Kynlee wasn't as restless about getting away from Reindeer Meadow.

They had done their Christmas shopping in Overland Park. No way anyone in Reindeer Meadow could have any idea what they were up to, just the way she wanted it. Kynlee had guessed at sizes for Greg and Amy Walters and purchased a few clothing items for them. She and Drake had splurged on gifts, toys for the kids. Kynlee had been thrilled to buy for her nephew—Tanner—and for Drake's niece, Addison, too.

She found she didn't mind Christmas music or wrapping paper when she was preparing a special Christmas for someone who needed it. Loaded with toys and a few necessary clothing items for the kids, she and Drake had gone to the grocery store and loaded up on staples for the Walters family, too.

They had taken it all to Kynlee's house in Reindeer Meadow, locked the doors, turned on Christmas movies, and wrapped everything but the grocery items. All that was left now was delivering the gifts without being caught by anyone in the family.

Without a sound, she and Drake climbed out of his truck. They pressed their doors closed carefully. If the Walters kids were like other kids, they might be awake inside, listening for Santa to come. Grabbing big red bags, just like Santa's, she and Drake carried them down the street to the tiny brick house. They had discussed earlier how to do the gifts—leave them in the bags or display them on the porch? Leaving the groceries out seemed problematic. What if animals raided those bags?

As they had decided, the two of them put the big red bags on the small porch and draped them open to reveal all the brightly wrapped red and green packages. When they finished, they stepped back and studied their work. Satisfied, they scurried back to the truck as quietly as they could. Each of them took a handle on the big cooler they had purchased for the grocery items. Because it was heavy, they moved slowly down the street this time and then carried it up over the driveway. They were careful to walk where someone—presumably Amy since Greg's back was still bad—had shoveled. When Drake stepped in snow and left a big boot print, Kynlee walked behind him and smoothed snow over the top the print to hide it.

They left the cooler to the side of the porch, easily visible from the front window and the door. Hand in hand, they headed back down the driveway. At the street, Kynlee stopped and turned back to look at the house again. Lights had been strung from the eaves, but several spots were dark where bulbs had gone out. An ancient-looking plastic Santa had been tipped over in the yard. And a snowman, made with muddy snow, half-melted already, stood guard at the end of the drive.

Kynlee made a silent wish that Greg Walters' back would improve so he could go back to work and take care of his family.

"Ready?" Drake whispered.

She nodded, and once again, they started walking toward the truck.

The cab was still warm, and adrenaline was still pumping through Kynlee like fire. Sweating now, she unzipped her coat and yanked the beanie off her head.

"So." Drake started the truck and eased it to the corner to make a right turn. "How do you feel?"

"Pretty incredible," she answered simply. "That was kind of a rush."

"It was," he agreed.

"Thanks for the idea," she told him as he steered his truck to her house. "Not sure why I didn't think of it sooner."

"You did. Just on a smaller level," he reminded her. "The day we met you took donuts to some high school girls, remember?"

She nodded and rested her head on the seat.

"You're okay with leaving tomorrow? To have dinner with my family?" he asked again.

"I am," she said softly. "I'm looking forward to it."

Drake pulled his truck into her driveway. Kynlee jumped out before he shut it off. She carried her beanie inside and unzipped her coat immediately. Drake stomped his feet on the mat outside her door before coming inside.

"One more Christmas movie?" he asked her.

"As long as it's *Die Hard*, sure."

Kynlee hurried into the bedroom and changed into her fleece Christmas plaid pajamas. She washed her face, but in case she decided on a midnight Christmas cookie, she held off on brushing her teeth. The lamp in the living room was off; the only light in the room came from the Christmas tree and the TV.

"You look like my favorite present," Drake announced as she sank down to sit by him on the couch. "Just need a bow in your hair."

Kynlee snorted. "Not likely."

"Not likely to the bow? Or that you're my present?"

"The bow."

He nodded. "I can deal with that."

He aimed the remote at the TV, but Kynlee glanced at the Christmas tree again.

"Drake! Shoot!"

"What?" He dropped the remote and looked at her. "What's wrong?"

"We forgot a present."

"No way."

"Seriously." She groaned as she climbed off the couch again and hurried around to the tree. One small box sat under the tree. Kynlee squatted down and reached for it. Wrapped in silver paper with a tiny white bow, the tag on it simply said *To Kynlee.*

She swallowed hard and looked at Drake, who had turned to sit backwards on the couch.

"We said no gifts. Remember?"

He huffed out a sigh and flinched.

"It's just one."

"But I don't want to do this. This isn't what it's about—"

Drake crawled to the end of the couch, climbed off, and came around to sit by her. He put his arms around her and pulled her into his lap.

"Just open it."

Heart in her throat, Kynlee pulled the bow off the gift and carefully unwrapped the box. She loved him. He had told her he loved her last spring, May twenty-sixth, to be exact.

They had been as inseparable as they could be while being in a long-distance relationship.

Kynlee was willing to pack up and move with him anywhere. She would say *I do* if he asked. But she didn't want gifts, especially not a ring. She had even told him if they ever got married, she wanted only a simple wedding band.

Her fingers trembled a bit as she pulled the top off the box. Nestled in white tissue paper inside the box was a glass ornament in the shape of a star.

"Flip it over." Drake's voice rumbled in her ear. Holding her breath, she picked the ornament up with care and looked at the back side of it. Her eyes burned with happy tears when she read the engraved words.

Kynlee & Drake

2023.

WISHING FOR LOVE SERIES

A December Wish is part of the WISHING FOR LOVE collaborative series hosted by Amaryllis Media.

Wishing for Love

Join us where holiday magic grants love to those pure of heart as love blooms and dreams come true during the most wonderful time of the year.

Escape into a world of pure holiday romance full of festive cheer and twinkling lights to warm your heart and leave you longing for more.

We hope you enjoy falling in love with our world as you follow along with these charming characters and the stories they share with us.

SNEAK PEEK AT EGGNOG IN AMESBURY

Chapter 1

McKenzie

Traffic on this highway was nonexistent. Good thing for her. McKenzie Noble had belted out the last four songs at the top of her lungs. She would be exhausted by the time she reached Amesbury. Not that she cared. A music fan in general, she *loved* Christmas music. And why not blare it if she was alone in her rental car on the drive? No one to complain about her singing off-key, and no one to pass her and notice her Grammy-Award winning concert.

She checked the time again. When she landed in Billings, she had been worried she would be late for this meeting. A heavy blanket of dark, mean-looking clouds hung low in the sky, but so far, only tiny flakes of snow fell, adding to that already on the ground here in Montana. The highway itself was clear, so as long as those clouds held off cutting loose with their fury until she reached Amesbury, she would be okay.

Three weeks into her new job, she couldn't afford messing anything up. The position at Inovial Educational Consulting was her first *real* job, as her younger brother would say, even though she had graduated from college six years ago. While she didn't mind waitressing, and yes, she had made good tip money, McKenzie was aware that her parents hadn't put her through college to work at Creighton's for the rest of her life.

Her mom had balked at the idea of her flying to Billings by herself, but McKenzie was thrilled at the opportunity. Not to mention, she was twenty-seven years old and had lived on her own since she had left home for college. The scouting trip, as her boss Lena had called it, was a perfect chance for her to prove herself at work and an opportunity to see Montana—more than what she had seen in the ridiculously popular TV show, *Yellowstone*.

Now, if she happened to run into a good-looking cowboy or two while she was here, she wouldn't complain. But she wasn't on the lookout for one, either. McKenzie wanted the traditional life her mom had; she wanted to get married and have kids. But right now, she needed to focus on her career. Maybe once she was settled at IEC, she would take time for dating again.

Elvis' version of "Blue Christmas" was her favorite, so naturally, when it started playing around her, she had to clear her throat and join in. She glanced at the dash, at what was basically a computer screen—and they wondered why people had accidents on the road— to consult the GPS. Ten more miles and she would be in Amesbury. According to the time on the dash, she had plenty of time to get checked into the resort and walk around the little ski town before her meeting.

She couldn't wait to see the place decked out for the holidays. Her brother, Christian, was the exact opposite. Hated snow, winter, Christmas—anything that wasn't stifling heat and sunshine and even soupy humidity. McKenzie used to wonder if she and Christian were adopted because they had such different ideas and interests. The question was ridiculous as she was a spitting image of her dad, and Christian of their mom. But she figured someday, when they were older and had their own families, she would be living somewhere with real seasons, leaves that changed colors in the fall, and white Christmases while Christian would be living somewhere beachy, where the only thing white about Christmas was the sand.

When she saw the billboard welcoming her to Amesbury— the pretty winter scene definitely made her feel cozy and welcome—she tapped her brakes with a glance in the rearview mirror. There was a car so far behind her she couldn't make out what it was, but other than that, nobody around. If she weren't the chipper, adventurous type that all her teachers had always noted on her report cards, she might find the lack of traffic, people, a little creepy. Instead, it only added to her hopes for a Hallmark-like atmosphere in this little Montana town.

McKenzie laughed at the thought of sending Snaps to her brother. Hopefully, she would find cutesy, over-the-top holiday stuff to photograph like streetlights wrapped in silver garland and a Christmas tree farm with a hot chocolate stand draped with fairy lights and maybe even a Santa with rosy cheeks and a big belly. Oh yeah, if she saw anything of the kind while she was in Amesbury, she would unload on Christian! It would be a fun payback for the pictures he had sent from Miami last year. The joke was on him, though. McKenzie loved Christmas, but she didn't mind pictures of the ocean and the beach.

She signaled as she took the Amesbury exit, singing along with Otis Redding now to "Merry Christmas Baby." She couldn't sit still, so she was dancing in her seat with what she knew had to be a big, dopey grin on her face. Her first glance at the small town took her breath away.

Main Street was beautiful. Quaint little businesses lined both sides of the street—an auto garage, restaurants, a coffee shop. McKenzie squealed softly as steered the SUV slowly down the street. She loved it here already. As soon as she got checked in at the lodge, she would text Lena and tell her about her first impressions of Amesbury.

ABOUT THE AUTHOR

Tracy Broemmer is the author of several contemporary romance novels including the 515 Whiskey Series, Shameless Santa, and the Mississippi Queen Trilogy. Tracy also writes women's fiction and is the author of the Williams Legacy series as well as several stand-alone titles.

Tracy's books have been called gripping, emotional, and timely, and readers describe her characters as real and relatable

Tracy lives in Midwestern Illinois with her husband of 30 years. Visit her on the web and sign up for her newsletter at www.broemmerbooks.com

ALSO BY TRACY BROEMMER

Women's Fiction Novels:

Luther's Cross (10th Anniversary Edition)

Fairytale (Writing as Therese Kinkaide)

Just Like Them

Small Hours

Picket Fences

Two Story Home

Green-Eyed Girl

Say Everything

Come Home for Christmas

Sketching Litchfield Lake

Ever, Again

Safe as Houses

Damsel

The Valentine Suite

Women's Fiction Series in Order

Lorelei Bluffs

Every Little Thing

Two A.M.

Blind

Leaving July

Hesitation Marks

Four Letter Words

See Kate

Loved You More

A Lorelei Ending

I Do

The Williams Legacy

Truth Is

Other People's Ugly

Omissions

Women's Fiction Short Stories

India Falls

Luther's Cross: 87,600

The Candy Cane Tree of Willow Lane

Delays

Same Time Next Year

Contemporary Romance Novels

Destiny's Calling: Your Future is Waiting

Wedding Day Shenanigans

Holiday Fling

The Kiss Off

Something Like Love

Plus One

End in Flames

Contemporary Romance Series In Order

The Mississippi Queen Trilogy

Love, Nashville

Forever, Duncan

Always, Jess

Truly, Dante (A Short Story)

The H Books

Gettin' Hitched

Hookin' Up'

Holdin' On (A Novella)

Timberton Hounds (Novellas)

Priceless Memory (A Short Story)

Endless Summer

Homeless Holiday

Restless Hearts (Currently included in Fall Into Love, an anthology by Fluffy Fox Publishing)

515 Whiskey

Intoxicate Me (A Novella)

Taste Me

Kissing Springs Trio

Shameless Santa

Sunshine & Soulmates

Bourbon & Bedposts

Lockland Distilling: Keys to Love Trilogy & Kissing Springs World

Leaving You (A Short Story)

Seducing You (A Novella)

Kissing You (A Novella—currently included in the Let's Get Naughty, Volume 2)

Shared World Novels

Hold Onto the Stars (Blue Collar Romance Series, Book #5)

The Jane Thing (Meet Cute Book Club Series, Book #2)

Shameless Santa (Welcome to Kissing Springs, Book #7)

Doctor Divine (Doctors of Eastport, Season 2)

Sunshine & Soulmates (Welcome to Kissing Springs, Book #

Bourbon & Bedposts (Welcome to Kissing Springs, Book #

Moonlight in Montreal (The Vagabond Series)

Beach Daze (Flamingo Island)

Christmas & Other Inconveniences (Betting on Christmas Collection)

Eggnog in Amesbury (Christmas in Amesbury)

Love in Motion Duet (Novellas)

Feels on Wheels

Rings on Wings

The Wine Tasting Series (Short Romantic Stories)

Perfect Pictures (Traminette)

Coming Home (Edelweiss)

Save Me Every Dance (Rosé)

Marry Me (Shiraz)

Birthday Wishes (Muscat)

Dad Jeans (Vignoles)

Contemporary Romance Novellas

Boone's Girl

Today, Again

Indian Summer

Dear Jaclyn Perris

Mistletoe Mishaps

Deadman's Hollow

French Stuff

Holdin' On

Toasted

End in Flames

Endless Summer

Homeless Holiday

Feels on Wheels

Rings on Wings

Intoxicate Me

Contemporary Romance Short Stories

Truest Love (Currently included in Show of Dreams anthology)

Swipe for Fangs (Currently included in the anthology Welcome to Whynot)

Mrs. Bennett

Peppermint Lane

The Principles of Accounting

Strawberry Wine

Love Letter

Sambuca Santa

Truly Dante

Leaving You

Priceless Memory

Perfect Pictures (Traminette)

Coming Home (Edelweiss)

Save Me Every Dance (Rosé)

Marry Me (Shiraz)

Birthday Wishes (Muscat)

Dad Jeans (Vignoles)

Other Novellas

The Devy Man, A Horror Novella

The Keeper's Heart, A Horror Novella

Anthologies

Just Coffee — French Stuff (2020)

Snowed Inn, Vol. 1 — Holdin' On (2020)

Aced, Back to School — Boone's Girl (2021)

Snowed Inn, Vol. 2 — Delays (2021)

Sweet Treats — Peppermint Lane (2021)

Sweet Sprinkles — Same Time Next Year (2022)

Rescue Me — End in Flames (2022)

Fall Into Love — Feels on Wheels (2022)

Cool Off — Endless Summer (2022)

Fall Back Into Love — Rings on Wings (2022)

Backing the Bluegrass — Leaving You (2022)

Kissing Santa Claus — Sambuca Santa (2022)

Let's Get Naughty — Homeless Holiday (2022)

XOXO — Trusting Cupid (2023)

Mrs. Right — Mrs. Bennett (2023)

Tease Me — Taste Me (2023)

Falling for the Boss — The Principles of Accounting (2023)

Ride a Cowboy — Seducing You (2023)

Love and Coffee — Makin' Whoopsie! (2023)

Fall Into Love — Restless Hearts (2023)

Welcome to Whynot — Swipe for Fangs (2023)

Let's Get Naughty, Volume 2 — Kissing You (2023)

Show of Dreams — Truest Love (2023)

www.ingramcontent.com/pod-product-compliance
Lightning Source LLC
Chambersburg PA
CBHW021203130626
46554CB00005B/1960